Verohica e Alex.

TO THE FOURTH GENERATION

Chick Yuill

Chick Yuill

*Still remember your
Kindness to us.*

instant apostle

Thanks!

First published in Great Britain in 2020

Instant Apostle
The Barn
1 Watford House Lane
Watford
Herts
WD17 1BJ

British Library Cataloguing-in-Publication Data

A catalogue record for this book is available from the British Library.

This book and all other Instant Apostle books are available from Instant Apostle:

Website: www.instantapostle.com

Email: info@instantapostle.com

ISBN 978-1-912726-26-4

Printed in Great Britain.

In memory of and in gratitude for:

my father
who really did march in the band every Sunday
despite fifty years of coal dust in his lungs
and who really did meet his brother
marching in the opposite direction

and

my mother
who really did sing with the songsters
and who really did make the finest chocolate
sponge
in all of Scotland

'Even the simplest story deals with more than one person, with more than one time. Characters begin young; they grow old; they move from scene to scene, from place to place ... Two words alone cover all that a writer looks at— they are, *human life* ... If you do not tell the truth about yourself you cannot tell it about other people.'
Virginia Woolf, The Leaning Tower: *a lecture delivered to the Workers' Educational Association, Brighton, May 1940*

'I, the LORD your God, am a jealous God, punishing the children for the sin of the parents to the third and fourth generation of those who hate me, but showing love to a thousand generations of those who love me and keep my commandments.'
Exodus 20:5-6 (NIVUK)

contents

chapter 1
the golden trowel

I've been telling stories all my life. That's what I do. That's what I've always done. It must have started with the squiggles and scribbled drawings I made of what I could see around me when I was very young. And as soon as I learned to speak – at least, that's how I remember it – I began to tell myself stories as I drifted off to sleep each night about what had happened that day. It was, I guess, my childish way of securing my place in the world – bringing things into focus, giving them some shape and colour, making sense of what was going on around me.

When I was five years old, I started school and discovered *letters*, those strange black characters that fascinated me and that I painstakingly copied onto lined paper until I could reproduce them perfectly. Then I learned to join them together to make words, words that could be written down on a page, formed into sentences and set in paragraphs. Words that could be used, not just to tell a story, but to *keep hold of it*, so that I could read it again and again and not forget it. Words, words, words. They fascinated me, became an obsession that got me into all kinds of trouble. My teachers shouted at me for daydreaming and not paying attention. My parents hid my pencil and notepad, hoping that would force me to 'live in the real world' and behave normally. By which they meant behave like the other kids. But the other kids knew better than the adults. The other kids knew instinctively that I was different. Sometimes they ignored me and carried on with their games, sometimes they regarded me with a detached and uncomprehending amusement, sometimes they teased me. But sometimes, if I showed them what I'd written, they'd get interested in my stories.

That's when I began to realise that telling stories wasn't just something you did for yourself. Even people who weren't exactly like *me* – people who didn't have the irresistible urge to make up their own stories – still wanted stories, wanted them as much as I did. They just needed someone else to find the stories, put them together, write them down. Other kids established their place in our competitive childhood world by being talented on the sports field, or smart with their schoolwork, or natural leaders, or better-looking than the rest of us. I carved out my own niche as the boy who could write stories. And, as I grew older and more confident, I learned that telling stories could have unanticipated outcomes.

When I was fifteen, I wrote a short story about our history teacher, known to us as Potty Potter. He was what from the perspective of adulthood I would now describe as an endearing eccentric. Back then, with the unthinking cruelty of youth, we just called him a *weirdo*, and he was the object of our endless and merciless ridicule. Mr Potter was a gentle, somewhat melancholy man who gave the impression that teaching was for him a wearying chore and that he would rather be anywhere else on earth than facing thirty fidgeting and distracted teenagers in a classroom. He must have been in his early sixties, short and tubby, with a shiny bald dome of a head circled by wisps of grey hair, a gap in his front teeth, glasses that were constantly slipping down his nose, a frequent twitch in his left eye, and a squeaky bicycle that he insisted on wheeling along the corridor and parking in the staffroom every morning, much to the annoyance of his fellow-teachers. Those were the facts. Everyone knew them. And I made good use of them in my tale. The more interesting bits of my story – the thirty-five-year-old former fashion model to whom he was married, his derelict house with no electricity or running water, his five children and six cats, and his previous life as the lead singer in a rock 'n' roll band – came straight from my imagination.

Ronnie Hobbs, the closest thing I had to a best pal in those days, read it and laughed until he couldn't get his breath. It deserved a wider audience, he insisted, and he knew how to reach that audience and make some money in the process. He managed to get into the photocopier room at lunchtime, run off a couple of hundred copies, and sell them to eager readers for 20p each. We shared the profits between us, although Ronnie, arguing that he'd done the real hard work of publishing and distributing this masterpiece of wit and satire, kept 85p from each pound for himself. However, when the three A4 photocopied pages covered in my instantly recognised handwriting inevitably ended up on the desk of our form teacher, I was the one who, as the author of the 'scurrilous tale', faced the ire of the headmaster and the threat of expulsion.

13

In the end, common sense prevailed and the severity of the punishment meted out to me was rather more proportionate to the gravity of the crime. I had to make a written apology to Mr Potter and acknowledge my wrongdoing before the entire school in the weekly assembly. The headmaster also informed me, in the sombre tones of a judge pronouncing a lengthy custodial sentence on a career criminal, that my name would definitely not be considered when they were choosing class prefects for the next school year. Since there had never been any likelihood of me being appointed to that exalted position anyway, to my mind that didn't really constitute a disciplinary procedure. The letter that was sent to my parents upset my mother and gave my father yet one more opportunity to tell me that it was time to stop retreating into a world of fantasy and fiction. Time to face the truth that the odds were stacked against me ever making a career out of writing.

'Buckle down and prepare yourself for a proper job,' he'd say, banging the table with his fist to emphasise the point. 'Nothing good ever comes from chasing unrealistic dreams.'

Despite the censure of the school authorities and the customary disapproval at home, that very first published story of mine – the first that people actually paid to read – brought a positive reaction from the most unexpected quarter. It was an encounter that would set the course of my life.

A couple of days after my public act of contrition, I was walking home from school on my own when I heard the sound of squealing brakes and a familiar figure on a bicycle pulled up beside me. It was Potty Potter. I braced myself for the torrent of angry condemnation that I was sure was about to roll over me. It never came. Instead, he got off his bike, shook his head and gave a slow half-smile, and fell into step with me. I'd have known how to deal with his anger. I'd no idea how to respond to this. I looked down at my feet and started to mumble an apology.

'It's alright, Binnie,' he said wearily. 'I'm not about to tell you off. I'm sure it's hard for you to believe, but I was your age once. And I'm not that old now that I don't remember making fun of teachers, though you *were* just a bit cruel.'

The unmistakable hurt in his voice left me in no doubt that what I'd written had bruised him. There was nothing I could say that would ease the situation and for the first time I felt the sickening bile of shame in my mouth. It was a bitter taste that I would experience more than once in the years to come.

He walked beside me without saying anything further for another two or three hundred yards until we reached the point where our paths diverged and he prepared to get back on his bicycle. He stopped for a moment and, as he began to speak again, the habitual look of weary resignation on his face changed. In all the hours I'd sat in his history class I'd never seen him with an expression like this. It remains as vivid in my mind's eye all these years later. His features came to life and his eyes lit up with a look of genuine interest and even hopefulness. It was as if some magic potion had instantly released him from a slumber-inducing spell that had kept him too long in its grasp.

'There's a reason I wanted to talk to you, Binnie.' Even his voice had lost its customary dreary monotone that

Ronnie Hobbs had imitated to such effect when selling my photocopied manuscript to our eager customers.

'Listen, lad. You can *write*. It's a pity you've never shown me that in any of the history assignments you've handed in to me.' There was just the hint of a chuckle when he said that, and I realised that I'd never actually heard him laugh before.

'Your story might have been more than a little unkind to me, but I'll be the first to admit that it shows signs of real talent. Now, don't waste that gift. I've been trying to be a writer all my life. I've worked hard at it. Got some of my stuff published. But I recognise *really* good writing when I read it. Even when it's a bit rough at the edges with too many nasty jibes and a few grammatical errors. From your recent effort at my expense, I suspect that you've got the potential to be a proper writer. Better than I'll ever be…'

He paused long enough to dig a brown envelope out of the bag that was slung over his shoulder and pushed it into my hand.

'You might want to read that,' he shouted as he began pedalling down the road that led off to the right. 'And it might help you to make better use of your talent.'

He rode off, a fat, short, bald man balancing precariously on his bike in a way that seemed to defy gravity. I stood stock still watching him make his slow and unsteady progress, and wondered what on earth had just happened and what I should make of it. I put the envelope in my satchel and began walking home feeling thoroughly confused.

It wasn't until I was getting ready for bed that night that I opened the envelope. I'd been putting it off because, for some reason I couldn't quite explain to myself, I was nervous about what I might find.

Inside were half a dozen pages paper-clipped together. At the top of the first page there was a couple of sentences in Mr Potter's handwriting: 'Binnie, you might find some of this interesting or even useful. Keep writing!'

I sat on the edge of my bed reading through the pages slowly and with growing interest. There was a photocopy of a short story he'd had published in a magazine I'd never heard of. But I guessed he'd chosen it deliberately because it was about a teacher who was the constant butt of his pupils' jokes but who managed to come out on top in the end. It was funny and clever and made me smile. The rest of the pages were filled with examples of well-written passages that he'd culled from a variety of sources and even some of his own observations on how to write well. I fell asleep that night thinking that I'd seriously underestimated my history teacher and resolved that I'd never call him Potty Potter again.

It was the beginning of a relationship that became a friendship to which I owe an unpayable debt. At first, from time to time he'd send me bits and pieces of helpful stuff he'd picked up in his reading. Then, when I discovered some other kids who had an interest in writing, we went to him and asked if he'd be willing to set up an after-school Writers' Club. He was initially reluctant, telling us that the demands of work and family left him with little time or energy for such activities. But we pressed him until, with the permission – not to mention to the relief – of the headmaster, who hoped this might be the means of transforming me into a model pupil, he agreed to our request.

Those late Friday afternoon meetings of seven or eight of us in Mr Potter's classroom formed the keystone of my education as a writer. And he was at his best. He lacked the assertive, larger-than-life personality to control and motivate a class of thirty pupils who had little or no interest in the subject he was employed to teach. Put him with a handful of enthusiastic students who were eager to learn, however, and he came alive. He became our rabbi and we his committed disciples who hung on his every word.

But I learned much more from him than how to begin my apprenticeship as a writer. In my last two years at school before I left for university, I got to know the man whom I had lampooned with all the insensitivity of a fifteen-year-old boy who thought he was clever but who knew nothing of real life. At Christmas he would invite the members of the Writers' Club to his home for an evening where we would each read a 500-word story we'd prepared for the occasion. That's when I discovered that his wife was not a former fashion model in her thirties, but a charming white-haired lady in her sixties who provided us with a supper that would have done justice to a major literary award ceremony. And he was father, not to five children, but to one physically and mentally disabled daughter called Amy who was in her thirties and to whose care he and his wife were devoted. They were as proud of her as they would have been of a daughter who was a talented athlete or a gifted scholar. The house in which they lived was humble but scrupulously clean and tidy and, above all, welcoming, a place in which I learned that many others had been the recipients of their generous hospitality. If there is any genuine humanity in the novels

I have written, it is all down to what I observed in the home life of Mr and Mrs Potter.

He was very proud when, at the Annual Prize-giving in my last year at school, I was presented with the inaugural William C Potter Short Story Award that he'd set up and funded to encourage young writers. I've been the recipient of a number of literary accolades over the years, but none of them has meant half as much to me as that first award. The certificate, embellished with his spidery signature, hangs above my desk to this day.

We kept in touch regularly after I'd left school and graduated from university until his death at the age of seventy when he was knocked off his bicycle by a speeding motorist. Even then, the link between us wasn't severed. His widow gave me the opportunity to take whatever books I wanted from his extensive library and entrusted me with all his papers and manuscripts. I've been earning a good living as a writer and novelist for years now. But without the encouragement of Mr Potter, a gentle and open-hearted man who saw past my teenage arrogance and encouraged my undeveloped talent, none of that would ever have happened.

It's more than two decades since his death, but I've been thinking about him more than ever recently and reflecting on one of the things he said to us over and over again until everyone in that group of youthful, would-be writers could repeat it like a mantra.

'Uncovering truth. That's the writer's main business,' he would tell us, looking at each one of us in turn. 'Not just giving the facts, but uncovering the truth. And your imagination is *the golden trowel*. Like the archaeologist's trowel, it will enable you to dig for the truth that lies just beneath the facts.'

In a few short years I'll hit fifty. I've had more success as a novelist than I ever dreamed possible. I could have retired by the time I was forty, never written another word, and I'd have had enough money to live comfortably. I might even have done so, had things not taken a sudden and unexpected turn. But living comfortably isn't enough. *I know that now, after what's happened*. It isn't the same as living... living how, exactly? I've spent my working days sitting with a pen in hand or in front of a keyboard trying to find precisely the right words that will capture my thoughts and communicate my meaning.

But I'm struggling to find the word that expresses what I want to say right now. The closest I can come is one that feels old-fashioned, flowery. One that isn't part of my normal vocabulary, either in my speaking or writing, but that's somewhere at the back of my mind from a visit I made to my grandparents in Scotland, a time that now seems very long ago. It's the word *abundantly*. I want to live life to the full. Break free from the prison I'm in. Find whatever it is I will need to walk free in the world and live a life that's generous to myself and to others. And I fear – no, I *know* – that I will never live such a life unless and until I examine the facts and uncover the truth that I've been afraid to look for – the truth about who I really am, the truth about *why* I am who I am, the truth about why I do what I do, the truth about what I have done and about what I haven't done. I've been putting it off for too long, maybe all my adult life, because I'm nervous about what I might uncover.

But I know it's time to take up the golden trowel that Mr Potter spoke about again and again. Of course, I want to handle the facts as carefully and as sensitively as an archaeologist would handle the stones and soil through which they were sifting so as not to damage the precious object they were seeking. So let me present the bare facts of my story. A story that's rooted in my family history.

I'm the fourth-generation male of my family to be named Alexander Binnie, though none of the first three generations were ever addressed by their legal name by those who knew them best. My great-grandfather entered the world on New Year's Day 1883. Growing up in the industrial belt of Scotland, he was known by everyone as Sandy, not only because that was a common abbreviation of Alexander in that time and place, but also on account of his shock of sandy-coloured hair. His oldest child, my grandfather, drew his first breath in 1903. Like his mother's brothers, he was taller than the average for that time and place and, at five feet ten, he stood a good three inches above his father. He also inherited his complexion and dark hair-colouring from his mother and thus avoided the fate of being the second Sandy in the family. Throughout his life he was known by the simple abbreviated form of the name, Alec.

My father was born in 1941. He favoured his grandfather in his colouring and in his physique. From childhood and through much of his adult life most people who've known him have referred to him as Ecky or even as 'Wee Ecky' – though rarely to his face, I should add – on account of his stocky muscular build. I arrived on the scene in 1971. Even before I reached my teens, according to my parents, it was clear that I was destined to be the tallest of the male line in the Binnie family. Since I'm just a touch over six feet, I console myself that there is at least one part of my destiny that I've fulfilled. At my mother's insistence I was always called Alexander at home. Everyone else abbreviated that to Alex and that's how I was known well into my twenties. My publishers, however, weren't persuaded that Alex Binnie looked sufficiently impressive on the cover of a book. So, for professional reasons, I became Zander Bennings and, to be honest, I rather like how that sounds. It's got a ring of confidence and competence with just the right touch of sophistication. And that, of course, is how my readers and the public know me. It's become so much part of my identity that some years ago I changed to that name by deed poll. Now even those closest to me, apart from my parents, never think to call me anything other than Zander.

I give you that brief genealogy because in order to uncover the truth about myself, I will have to tell the truth as accurately as I can about *them*. If changing my name to Zander Bennings emphasises the distance between me and those three generations that have gone before me, there are other things that go much deeper than a change of name, things that link my story to theirs, things that have made us what we are and things that have stopped us being what we might have been.

We are bound together by cords even stronger than ties of blood. I cannot tell you *my* story truthfully without telling you *their* story as accurately as I can. I need to take that golden trowel that Mr Potter recommended to us and dig carefully and imaginatively into the story of my family and my relationship with that family. Only then, I suspect, will it be possible to expose the truth, the reality that would otherwise remain hidden just beneath the surface...

past

chapter 2
marching as to war
1914–16

Sandy Binnie knew nothing of the complex geopolitics of Europe in the early years of the twentieth century. The bewildering tangle of ever-changing alliances and never-ending quarrels between empire-building nations jockeying for power and prestige on the other side of the English Channel meant little to him. Even the newspaper headlines a couple of months previously, informing the people of Britain of the assassination of Archduke Franz Ferdinand of Austria by the nineteen-year-old Bosnian Serb nationalist, Gavrilo Princip, attracted only his passing interest. It was a tragic and senseless murder, certainly. But such dark deeds in faraway countries involving people with strange-sounding foreign names were of no lasting concern to a young man trying to make his way in the industrial belt of Scotland, a young man with a wife and children, a young man who felt that life was just beginning and for whom the future was full of promise.

At a quarter past twelve on this day, however, his mind was filled with pressing matters that required his immediate action. Normally at the close of the service, having marched his Boys' Brigade company smartly out of the church and made sure that each lad had been returned to the care of his parents, he would have gone straight home with his family for lunch. But Sunday 13th September 1914 was definitely not a normal Sunday for Sandy Binnie. Today he knew exactly what his duty was and what had to be done. He made a hasty excuse to his wife about having to attend an unexpected meeting before heading for a side door where two of his fellow Boys' Brigade leaders, both of them some years younger than him, were waiting to follow his lead. The three of them stood for a moment, shook hands with each other to affirm their commitment to the action they'd agreed on, pushed their Glengarry bonnets firmly on their heads, and strode purposefully out of the church. They caught a bus into Glasgow and then walked briskly for ten minutes through the streets of the city, laughing and chatting excitedly until they turned on to George Street and found themselves standing in front of the imposing sandstone edifice that was their destination.

They pushed open the heavy ornate door and entered the spacious hallway of the Glasgow Technical College. A message chalked on a blackboard directed them to a gloomy passageway where they took their places sitting on long wooden benches behind fifty or sixty other young men, two-thirds of whom were also dressed in the same Boys' Brigade uniform. One by one, those at the head of the queue were summoned through a door at the far end of the corridor. It was a wearingly slow process and the clock had struck three in the afternoon before the summons came to Sandy Binnie. A soldier, whom he

28

guessed was a few years younger than himself, beckoned him into a room where a man in his fifties with an impressive waxed military moustache sat behind a desk with a large stack of papers on his right-hand side. Without bothering to look up, he slid a sheet of paper from a smaller pile on his left and poised, pen in hand, ready to write.

'Name,' he said abruptly.

'Alexander John Binnie,' came the slightly nervous reply.

The recruiting sergeant glanced up from the desk with an expression that changed instantly from boredom to irritation.

'Alexander John Binnie, *sir*!' He shouted that last word at the eager but anxious would-be soldier standing in front of him. 'We've a war to win, young man, and we need soldiers who understand respect and discipline. I would have thought your Boys' Brigade experience would have taught you that. Now, what's your age and present employment?'

The chastened volunteer apologised for his failure to address his interviewer in a fitting military manner and replied that, having been born on the 1st of January 1883, he was thirty-one years old and had worked as a grocer's assistant since leaving school. He could see immediately from the manner in which the officer sitting in front of him sniffed dismissively and shook his head that his profession was one for which he had nothing but contempt.

'Well, the army will give you some real work. We might even manage to make a man of you.'

He moved quickly on to a series of routine questions before adding the sheet of paper on which he'd been writing to the stack of papers on his right, pointing to a man in a white coat standing at the far end of the room, and shouting, 'Binnie, Alexander John: put him through the medical and check his eyesight.'

The perfunctory medical examination lasted no more than ten minutes. The formalities of signing his name and enlisting took even less time. And by six o'clock that evening the Boys' Brigade leader, now a prospective private in Field Marshall Lord Kitchener's army, was back in the *single end*, the one-roomed dwelling that he proudly and gratefully called home, sharing his usual Sunday tea-time meal of bread and jam and home-made biscuits with his wife, Peggy, and their two sons, Alec and Bobby. Despite his wife's curiosity as to where he'd been all afternoon, he waited until the boys had been settled down for the night and the curtain had been drawn across the recessed hole-in-the-wall bed where they slept. Only when he was sure they were soundly asleep did he tell her what he'd done earlier that day. She was shocked by the news that in less than two weeks he would be reporting for duty with the Second Battalion of the Highland Light Infantry.

'Why do *you* have to go?' she asked tearfully. 'You told me yourself that you're doing well at work. They've talked about making you assistant manager. And the boys will really miss you.'

He looked up at the calligraphed, framed copy of the *Object of the Boys' Brigade* that was hanging on the wall above the fireplace:

The advancement of Christ's kingdom among Boys and the promotion of habits of Obedience, Reverence, Discipline, Self-respect and all that tends towards a true Christian manliness.

'It's right there, Peggy,' he said quietly, making sure his voice didn't disturb their sleeping children. 'We're at war and it's only right for me to serve my king and country. It's the *manly* thing to do. It's the *Christian* thing to do. I've been teaching those things to the lads in my company. If I stayed at home, I'd be a hypocrite.'

The household chores that normally occupied the last hours of a Sunday were forgotten as they contemplated the challenges that the future might bring. They sat quietly until the daylight began to fade, holding hands and feeling no need to say more than a few words to each other. It was ten o'clock by the time Sandy carefully eased their mattress from under the bed where the boys were now fast asleep, unrolled it and covered it with a sheet and blankets. Then, before lying down on their makeshift bed on the floor, husband and wife knelt to pray as they always did last thing at night by the armchair they'd inherited from Peggy's parents. They thanked God for the blessings of the day, sought his forgiveness for any wrongs they might have done, and asked for His presence and protection through the night.

'We'll be alright,' Sandy assured his wife as he extinguished the flickering gas light. 'Our faith has been enough for us in the past. It'll see us through these days.'

That was all he needed to say and all that Peggy needed to hear. They slept surprisingly soundly, secure in their simple trust in such eternal certainties.

Two weeks later, Private Alexander Binnie was living under canvas in the Ayrshire village of Barassie. As autumn began to give way to the chill of an early Scottish winter, the bracing wind that blew in from the east shore of the Firth of Clyde sharply reminded him that the comforts of the life he'd known, such as they were, had been left behind. Despite his longing for home and family, those early days of military service were not without their consolations. He was confident that he was doing what was right as a loyal citizen and a faithful Christian. And the repeated assurances of the men around him that 'with a bit of luck it might all be over by Christmas' gave him hope that his soldiering days might be a brief and uneventful interlude before he resumed his normal life. Most of all, he enjoyed the comradeship of the other volunteers. So many of his fellow Boys' Brigade officers had enlisted that the Second Battalion of the Highland Light Infantry quickly became known as *The Boys' Brigade Battalion* or, less respectfully by some cynics, as *The Holy Second*. It was a great relief to him that he hadn't found himself in what had equally swiftly been labelled *The Boozy First*, a battalion made up of hard-drinking, working-class Glaswegians whose company he would certainly not have found so conducive.

The oft-repeated prediction that hostilities would last no more than a few months turned out to be one of the most inaccurate prophecies ever made. As the weeks passed into months and 1914 slipped into 1915, the battalion moved south and Private Sandy Binnie, who'd never before travelled distances of more than forty or fifty miles, found himself in places far from home. From a camp that he was told was in Shropshire – though it seemed to him to be in the middle of nowhere – they relocated first to a village on the outskirts of Sheffield for firing practice, then on to Wensleydale on the east side of the Pennines for further training, before proceeding to Salisbury Plain where they linked up with the two other battalions that had been formed in Glasgow – *The Boozy First*, who were doing their best to live up to their description, and the equally appropriately nicknamed *Feather Bed Third*, so called because their numbers comprised mostly middle-class professional men whom senior military leaders hoped would be officer material and who consequently were living in comparative luxury compared to their less-favoured brothers-in-arms.

If the good-natured banter and the peaceful rural settings in which the naïve volunteers found themselves in those early days had lulled them into a mistaken sense that this would be a brief but happy adventure from which they would soon return home to regale their loved ones with interesting tales, they were quickly disillusioned. A few weeks later they were on the move again, this time to Southampton where they were each given the additional equipment of a life jacket before being herded onto a crowded ship in the middle of the night. Nine hours later, almost a thousand men, most of whom had never previously been to sea, and half of whom were violently seasick, disembarked unsteadily at Le Havre on the Normandy coast. Within a couple of days, they were heading north-east on a slow, dreary railway journey in cramped and cold cattle trucks. Their uncomfortable transport eventually came to a halt at the end of the track near the town of Amiens.

That was when the marches started. And that was when they began to understand what being soldiers in the British Army really involved. The train journey had meant long periods of unrelieved boredom, but the discomfort of trudging for seemingly endless hours was enough to make them yearn for the relative ease of the crowded cattle trucks from which they'd been so glad to escape. Trudging up to eighteen miles a day on roads jammed and blocked with all kinds of heavy military traffic would have been tiring enough in itself. Carrying the kit with which each man had been provided – rifle and bayonet, ammunition, spare boots, blankets, waterproof sheet, holdall bag, canteen and basic cutlery – made it an exhausting exercise for which they were ill prepared. Once every hour they were allowed to halt for five minutes' rest. The first instinct was to lie down at the roadside, but wiser heads quickly learned to resist that temptation. The weight of the kit they were carrying made it all but impossible to get up again without help from others and the effort involved in standing to their feet meant that beginning to walk again required an almost superhuman effort and only increased the weariness they already felt.

After several days of marching, they arrived in the village of Bouzincourt, just a few miles behind the trenches on the frontline, where they camped and rested for four days. Private Sandy Binnie, utterly fatigued by the exertions of the previous weeks, woke early on the first morning having managed to sleep for more than five hours despite the constant noise of the military vehicles that rumbled past throughout the night. It was already light and he made his way to the long pit that was filled with stagnant mud and equipped with large biscuit tins where he relieved himself at the hastily constructed latrine. There was a nauseating stench of human excrement mixed with the pungent odour of chloride of lime. Unable to find any clean water with which to wash, he spat on his hands and tried to wipe them with a rag he pulled from his pocket in a futile attempt to clean them. He looked at his grimy fingers and a feeling of utter revulsion, the like of which he'd never experienced before, swept over him. Tears welled up in his eyes as he longed for the safety of home, for the love of Peggy and the boys, and for the blissfully ordinary routine of life in the grocer's shop where he always wore a crisp white freshly laundered apron and his hands were always clean.

He was rubbing the back of his arm across his face to dry his tears when something glinting in the distance caught his eye. He squinted in the morning sun, unable to distinguish exactly what he was looking at, when a corporal about his own age came alongside him.

'You've seen it too, Binnie? Strange sight, i'n'it. Some of us noticed it yesterday afternoon when we got here.'

'What on earth is it?'

'It's a golden statue of the Virgin Mary. And she's holding the baby Jesus above her head. Don't ask me why she's doing that, but it's on the top of the cathedral in Albert, less than a couple of miles from here. A bit of a local landmark apparently. Seems the German artillery had a pop at it a few weeks ago which has left the whole thing leaning over at a crazy angle. Nobody can understand why it's still managing to hang on.'

The corporal patted him on the back good-naturedly.

'Wouldn't be surprised if we all end up a bit like that, Binnie, before this bloody war is over.'

He hurried off with a wry chuckle, leaving Sandy to ponder the bizarre sight. The corporal's words disturbed him even though they'd been intended as nothing more than a light-hearted comment. His Scottish Presbyterian upbringing had instilled in him an instinctive suspicion of religious icons, but there was something about the sight of the wounded Madonna and Child that moved him. Something that troubled him deeply. He'd enlisted in the conviction that he would be playing his part in a battle in which right was certain to triumph over wrong. But what if victory was not certain? What if everything he'd believed since childhood was *not* as straightforward as he'd imagined? He'd seen enough since crossing the English Channel to disabuse him of his idealistic notions of life as a soldier. The further they'd marched into France, the coarser and more bawdy the conversation of many of his fellow-soldiers had become. The easy banter of those first nights under canvas often gave way to cursing and blaspheming. Arguments and fights sometimes flared up among the men as tiredness drained the strength from their bodies and the truth of what they'd let themselves in for took shape in their minds. Maybe, as the corporal had implied, they'd all end up with their humanity and decency shattered. Maybe even *he* would end up with his hitherto unquestioned faith as broken and skewed as the statue that was hanging so precariously and uncertainly from the basilica he could just make out in the distance.

He turned away and hurried back to get his equipment together ready for the next stage of their march to the front, telling himself that these were just dark thoughts, inevitable temptations to doubt and despair that could be overcome with regular prayer and an effort of the will.

But, as he fell into step with his comrades on their way to the front line, he knew that something in him had changed for ever that morning. It was less than six months since he'd kissed his wife and his two boys goodbye and assured them of his safe return. Now he suspected that if he was fortunate enough to come out of this alive, he would go home a very different man from the one who'd set out with his confidence high and his simple faith intact.

Just a few weeks of front-line soldiering was more than long enough for him to discover just how much things had altered and how radically he was being changed. Nothing in his previous life or in his military training had prepared him for the sheer soul-destroying discomfort of life in the trenches. The filthy mud and water that permanently swilled around his ankles meant that he suffered terribly from trench foot. His feet would swell, become completely numb and, when they eventually recovered some sensation, the agony of the returning feeling would be unbearable. The nagging fear that it might lead to gangrene, as it had done with some of the men around him, contributed to a near-constant and exhausting state of anxiety. Rats, some as big as domestic cats, were an ever-present menace. It required an unceasing vigilance to ensure they didn't gnaw through his ration bag, though it was a standing joke among the men that the bully beef, dry bread and rock-hard biscuits that formed their staple diet were more suited to vermin than humans. Then there was the excruciating itching from the lice that infested the trenches and made their home on every soldier forced to serve there. His previously cheerful personality was slowly but surely submerged in repeated waves of irritability and resentment.

Everything else was a mixture of boredom – long days spent doing nothing but waiting, filling a few sand bags to shore up the trench, or writing letters home to reassure Peggy that 'things aren't too bad' – interspersed with periods of intense danger – the ping of a sniper's rifle or the terrifying noise of a shell from a German field gun whizzing through the air only to be followed by the unmistakable thud as it landed somewhere too close for comfort. Even the rhythm of combat that was intended to provide some semblance of rest and the opportunity to recuperate – four days in the front-line trenches broken up by some time in the reserve trench or in the rest camp behind the front line – offered little respite. The sounds of battle, just a couple of miles away, made sound sleep all but impossible and the knowledge that he would have to return to the fighting was never far from his mind. What made things even worse for Sandy was the sense of guilt and hypocrisy that stalked him relentlessly. His awareness of soldiers who made no profession of faith, but who coped with the pressures of life at the battle's front with a stoic acceptance and an enviable good humour, served only to highlight his own inability to deal with the pressures. He was forced to the conclusion that either he was a very poor Christian or everything he claimed to believe was meaningless. Or, even worse, both conclusions were right.

The end of his time as an active soldier came on a July morning just over a year later. The previous evening, when the battalion had moved up to the front line following intensive training, Private Sandy Binnie had carefully written a letter to his wife, parcelled it up with a few personal belongings, and carefully addressed the package to Mrs Peggy Binnie, 15 Calder Road, Bellmill, Lanarkshire, Scotland. He handed it, with the request that it should be sent to her if he didn't survive the next day's battle, to the corporal who'd pointed out to him the damaged Madonna and Child tilting so incongruously from the top of the cathedral in Albert. So much had happened since then. It seemed a lifetime ago since that morning shortly after his arrival in France. But he'd never been able to get that image out of his mind. Everything about his broken life – his faith, his confidence in himself as a man, his place in the world as a husband and father – was summed up in that image of the shattered icon, barely clinging on to the pedestal mounted high above the cathedral. The only thing of which he was now certain as he drifted off to sleep that night was that he would have to accept whatever fate might decree for him in the battle that awaited him in a few hours.

At exactly 7.30am on Saturday 1st July 1916, each man having been fortified by a larger than usual tot of rum, the order was given to advance. The Battle of the Somme had begun. The men of the Second Battalion of the Highland Light Infantry followed each other on to the fire-step and climbed up the short ladders propped against the wall of the trench that took them over the parapet and into the hell of No Man's Land. They walked slowly and deliberately as they'd been instructed, taking care to avoid the deep craters made by the enemy shells that had been blasted in their direction for many days. The unnatural silence that greeted the first troops over the top lasted for only a moment or two before the quiet was shattered by the sound of rapid machine-gun fire and the deafening noise of exploding shells all round them. Within a short time, the bodies of British soldiers, both wounded and dying, littered the battlefield.

Sandy Binnie just kept walking, his bayoneted rifle at the ready, with no real sense of where he was supposed to be going or what the point of the exercise was meant to be. The soldier to his right, whom he'd met and spoken to in the corridor of the Glasgow Technical College when they'd enlisted and whom he knew only by his first name, was hit in the face by an explosive bullet. Sandy looked with a horrified fascination at the sight of the man's jaw hanging loose. He knew that it shouldn't be like that, and somewhere in the back of his mind the thought began to form that he should do something to help relieve the man's suffering. But he could neither figure out what was to be done nor summon up the energy to do it. All he could do was to continue steadily and mechanically picking his way through the carnage until he became aware of a searing pain in his right leg. He glanced down to discover that his trousers were torn and saturated with blood. He stood still, staring at the gaping wound and wondering what to do next. Then he lost consciousness.

chapter 3
what dark shadow
1918

On Saturday 23rd November 1918, less than two weeks after the armistice had been signed, David Lloyd George, the man acclaimed by popular opinion as 'the leader who'd won the war', stepped confidently on to the stage to the enthusiastic applause of an expectant and capacity audience. Canny politician that he was, he sensed there was no better place than among the foundries and collieries of the Black Country and no better time than this moment, when the nation was still basking in the warm afterglow of victory, in which to launch his bid to be re-elected as Prime Minister of the United Kingdom of Great Britain and Northern Ireland. Experience told him that this was an occasion on which his seductive Welsh vowel-sounds and his persuasive oratory, practised and honed over a lifetime of public speaking, would cast a spell over his hearers and resonate far beyond the walls of Wolverhampton's Grand Theatre. He posed the question of what the next task should be for a country victorious in war but broken and exhausted by four years of conflict. It was a question for which he had his answer prepared and ready. And he would deliver that answer in words that would not quickly be forgotten.

'To make Britain a fit country for heroes to live in.'

He waited for the ripple of applause and the murmur of approving comments that rolled up like a wave from the body of the hall to subside before he continued.

'I am not using the word "heroes" in any spirit of boastfulness, but in the spirit of humble recognition of fact. I cannot think what these men have gone through. I have been there at the door of the furnace and witnessed it, but that is not being in it, and I saw them march into the furnace. There are millions of men who will come back. Let us make this a land fit for such men to live in.'

Sandy Binnie read the report of the Prime Minister's words the following afternoon and tossed the newspaper across the room in disgust. He was certainly one of those who had marched into the furnace and come back. But he had not returned unscathed. He was reminded of his hurts every time he looked at the stump of his right leg or struggled to attach the clumsy and uncomfortable prosthetic limb with which he'd been provided when he was invalided out of the British Army. The long months spent lying in a military hospital had given him more time to think and reflect than he would have wished. His memory of the day his leg had been shattered by flying shrapnel was confused and hazy. What he could never forget, however, was the terror that he'd struggled to suppress as he'd gone over the top and made his way through the desolation of No Man's Land. In truth, it was more of a horrifying re-enactment of the experience rather than just a memory of something that had happened in his past. And it could engulf him at any hour of the day. There

42

were few nights when his sleep was not invaded by hideous dreams of exploding shells and severed limbs. Vivid nightmares would cause him to wake sweating and shaking at the scenes of human carnage from which he could never escape.

He constantly struggled to free himself from these episodes that threatened to take control of him. He desperately wanted to be grateful to the men who'd somehow managed to carry him to safety from the battlefield and who'd saved his life at the risk of their own. He recognised the painstaking care given to him by the doctors and nurses, mostly young men and women, who were struggling with the overwhelming demands being made on their limited medical experience and the stretched resources at their disposal. He acknowledged that he was one of the lucky ones. *He was alive.* Political leaders might be reluctant to reveal or even face the shocking truth of the human cost, but anyone who'd been there knew beyond doubt that the toll of dead and injured soldiers, even on the first day of the Battle of the Somme, must have been catastrophic. But whatever he tried to tell himself, his overpowering emotions were those of frustration and resentment. 'Hero' was the last word he would have used to describe himself. He'd been scared most of the time. He'd contributed nothing of any significance to the war effort. *And he'd come back only half a man.* A one-legged cripple who'd never again be the husband and father he'd been when he'd made his way to the Glasgow Technical College with such naïve idealism four years before. And whether Britain would prove to be a land fit for heroes, only time would tell. But if he'd been a betting man, he wouldn't have risked a penny on such a utopia materialising in his lifetime.

He drew a deep breath, took himself to task for succumbing to such dark thoughts yet again, and pushed on the arms of the chair to raise himself into a standing position. As he steadied himself on one leg and reached for the crutch he kept always by his side, Peggy came back into the room from the outside washhouse where she'd spent the morning doing the week's laundry.

'Good,' she said encouragingly. 'You're up and moving. You'll feel all the better for getting out of the house. I'm sure they'll offer you something worthwhile today. They might even want to give you your old job back. You could still become the assistant manager.'

He gave her a half-smile and shook his head.

'Hmph… we'll see. But I wouldn't get your hopes up too much if I was you. Four years is a long time. Things have moved on. And Tommy Maxwell's a hard-nosed businessman. It won't have been easy keeping the shop going, and he's not about to get teary-eyed at the sight of one more ex-serviceman asking for a job.'

With the aid of the crutch, he hobbled to the kitchen where he heated a kettle for water to wash and shave before carefully attaching his artificial leg and slowly getting dressed. It was a process that he was still struggling to master and it was the first time he'd worn a suit since he'd come back home nearly four months ago.

'My, you look smart, Mr Binnie,' Peggy declared a little too enthusiastically as she helped him straighten his tie. She kissed him on the cheek. 'I'd certainly give you a job any day.'

He was amazed at how she'd changed since he'd enlisted in the army. His absence had forced her to become much more self-sufficient. In their earlier years of marriage, she'd depended on him for most things. But four years of running the home, having to find part-time employment to make ends meet, and bringing up Alec and Bobby on her own, had given her a much greater self-assurance. He knew that this was one more thing for which he should be thankful. In his darker moments, however, her growing confidence was just something else that threatened his own increasingly fragile sense of self-worth.

'And you know I've still got my cleaning job,' she said, holding him by the shoulders and looking into his eyes. 'The boys are both earning a bit of money now. Neither of them wants to leave home yet. So we'll be alright. You don't have to worry, even if it takes a bit of time to find work.'

Her words were intended to reassure him, but they served only to increase the irritation he was already feeling. The whole idea of his wife having to go out to work was bad enough, adding as it did to his sense of guilt at failing to fulfil his role as the main breadwinner. And the mention of the boys' employment made him feel worse still. Since they'd been children, he'd hoped that they might aspire to something better than settling for a job in a grocer's shop as he'd done on leaving school. He'd encouraged them to avoid what he regarded as the slovenly speech of the children around them, to learn to speak in a way that would fit them for some kind of career. An office job or a proper trade, perhaps. Something with a secure future and prospects of promotion. To his dismay, he'd learned on his return from the war that they'd both found work in one of the local coalmines. The two boys were only a year apart in age. Bobby, who wasn't yet fifteen, was still doing maintenance jobs at the pit-head, but Alec had already been working underground for almost a year. The thought of them both going down into the blackness of a coalmine every day served only to deepen the preoccupation with danger and death that always hung over him.

It was only half a mile to Bellmill's Main Street, and Peggy tentatively suggested that she might go with him 'just for a bit of company'. He immediately declined her offer. The last thing he wanted, he told her curtly, was for people to think he needed someone to help him along the street. He'd be fine on his own. He slammed the door behind him and called out that she needn't worry as he set off with the uncertain gait of a man who was still learning how to walk again. Tommy Maxwell had agreed to see him when the shop closed for the evening and he set off in good time to be there just before half past five. Despite the chill of the grey November day, the effort of walking on his artificial leg dressed in his worsted serge suit and stiff collar left him sweating profusely. He reached the shop and paused to look up at the sign above the window – THOMAS MAXWELL & SON. High Class Grocer. It had been recently repainted in a bolder font and much brighter colours than when he'd worked there. Things had apparently moved on in the four years since he'd told his surprised and disappointed employer that he'd enlisted in the army and would be leaving in a week's time.

He waited a few yards down the street until he saw the last customer and the two afternoon shop assistants leave together before he pushed the door open and stepped unsteadily into the store. Even in the faint glow of the partially installed electric lighting he could see the shocked expression on the face of the man standing behind the counter.

'Good grief! It's *you*, Sandy. But your hair – it's almost white.' Tommy Maxwell quickly tried to regain his composure. 'I'm sorry. It's just… I didn't recognise you at first. I heard you'd had a hard time in France.'

He lifted the hatch on the counter and beckoned to Sandy to step through.

'Just drop the catch and put the closed notice on the door and come into the back where we can chat. I'm sure you still remember your way round the old place.'

They made their way to the far corner of the storeroom where they sat facing each other on the two familiar battered armchairs he remembered so well, and made small talk for five minutes. Everything looked just as it had done on the day he had left. The well-scrubbed floorboards. The desk where he knew Tommy sat at the end of each day to count the takings and get the money ready for the bank the next morning. The tidily stacked crates ready to be picked up when the next delivery was made. But it was the distinctive smells of the place – the old leather of the armchairs, cardboard boxes and the tantalisingly mixed aroma of a variety of foodstuffs – that released a wave of nostalgia and tricked him into thinking for a moment that nothing had really changed. All he'd just come through had been no more than an inconvenient and unpleasant interruption to life and everything could now return to normal. He allowed himself to savour the prospect of being involved in the daily routine of a busy shop again. That was when he heard the words, though they were spoken quietly and hesitatingly, that jolted him back to reality.

'Sandy, I'd love to be able to give you your old job back. But at the moment I just don't have a vacancy. We had to take on other people after you left, of course – good people, reliable workers – and it wouldn't be fair to get rid of them. We managed to keep things going during the war and the business is doing alright. But I went through our accounts again last night and I know we couldn't afford an extra wage right now. I'll certainly keep you in mind, though. Maybe in a year or so, when we see how things are working out, I can get in touch with you again. And you might be feeling stronger by then...'

Tommy Maxwell shifted uncomfortably in his chair and gave a self-conscious smile as his voice trailed away. Sandy realised immediately the import of the words and the significance of the speaker's awkward movements. His former employer was embarrassed by his presence and had no intention of offering a job to a man whom he considered no longer fit for regular work. But he kept up his side of the pretence by responding that he understood the situation and that he'd make contact again in another twelve months or so. But he knew he would never do that. He would never enter Tommy Maxwell's shop or beg for a job again. The two men shook hands, exchanged polite, meaningless pleasantries, and the conversation was at an end. As the door of the shop clicked shut behind him, something broke within Sandy Binnie. He walked a hundred yards along the street, stepped into an unlit doorway and cried tears of humiliation and anger.

It was well past ten o'clock when he reached home, supported by Alec and Bobby whom Peggy had sent out to look for him. It was only after hours of searching, and to their astonishment, that they'd found their father, whom they'd never known to touch alcohol other than when he'd made a hot toddy to combat a heavy cold, drinking with a group of other unemployed ex-servicemen in The King's Arms. His slurred speech rendered his attempted apology to his wife unintelligible. But she needed no explanation and she knew that night, as she lay beside his broken body listening to his deep breathing, that life with her husband would never be the same again.

chapter 4
the boys in the band
1926

The Main Street in the coalmining town of Bellmill was unusually busy for six o'clock on a Sunday evening. But Sunday 9th May 1926 was no ordinary Sunday. Five days earlier the Trades Union Congress had declared a General Strike throughout the nation. The unprecedented mass action had been called in support of the country's miners in their dispute with the mine owners who'd locked out more than a million of their workers because of their refusal to accede to the employers' demands that they should work longer hours for less money. Prime Minister Stanley Baldwin's plea to the strikers that they should trust him 'to ensure a square deal and to ensure even justice between man and man' had fallen on deaf ears. The angry men who'd gathered in groups at almost every corner were in no mood to listen to what they deemed to be the empty promises of a political leader whose wealth and privilege meant that he had neither understanding nor sympathy with the plight of the working classes.

There had already been skirmishes between police and strikers earlier in the day and the atmosphere was noticeably tense. The special policemen who'd been hurriedly drafted in to assist in guarding the peace followed nervously behind the regular officers as they walked past the groups of striking miners. It was a stand-off in which neither side was willing to back down and neither side was sure what would happen next. What did happen allowed a release of tension that, in the view of the headline article in the following morning's newspaper, might well have prevented the discontent of the strikers manifesting itself in a full-scale riot. At precisely the same moment, from opposite ends of the street, came two bands, each marching to the strains of very different music and each determined to convey a radically different message. From the crossroads at the southern end of the town came the Bellmill Communist Flute Band preceded by a plain red flag and followed by some fifty party members lustily singing their anthem of undying allegiance to their colours:

> Then raise the scarlet standard high,
> Beneath its folds we'll live and die.
> Though cowards flinch and traitors sneer,
> We'll keep the red flag flying here.

And from the opposite end of the road, marching behind their yellow, red and blue, 'Blood and Fire' banner, came the Bellmill Salvation Army Band. Behind them marched a regiment of men and women, some of whom had deserted the tap rooms of the local pubs to join their ranks and imbibe a different kind of spirit. Their song was no less of a battle hymn, though their understanding of the nature of the conflict in which they were engaged contrasted starkly with that of the procession coming towards them on the other side of the street:

> Onward Christian soldiers!
> Marching as to war,
> With the cross of Jesus
> Going on before.
> Christ, the royal Master,
> Leads against the foe;
> Forward into battle,
> See, His banners go!

To anyone unfamiliar with life in a Scottish working-class town in that time and place, the reaction of the men lining the street to these two companies of people with their contrasting views of life would have been astonishing. For spontaneously, as the two bands drew level and their music clashed discordantly, many of the onlookers broke into warm applause. Their appreciation, surprising as it might seem, was not entirely without reason. If they didn't fully share the convictions of either group, they nonetheless respected the willingness of both to commit to a cause and their readiness to express their convictions in service to their community. They were understandably suspicious of many of the more extreme positions taken up by their Communist neighbours, but they were nonetheless grateful for the fact that they were frequently the first to take a stand against the establishment when issues of fairness and justice were at stake. And their willingness to poke fun at the Salvationists who frequently interrupted their Saturday evening pint with a pointed question about their eternal destination and a pressing invitation to purchase a copy of *The War Cry* was equally understandable. But it was tempered by an ungrudging respect and a ready recognition that the religious fervour of the men and women in Salvation Army uniforms went hand in hand with a practical concern for the poorest and neediest in their town.

The good-natured response was particularly vociferous among a knot of miners standing on the pavement when they spotted two of their workmates from the Black Moss Colliery who were marching in opposite directions. They cheered and clapped enthusiastically when one of the cornet players in The Salvation Army Band lowered his mouthpiece from his lips and nodded to the man playing the bass drum in the Communist Flute Band who returned his greeting with a wave of his drumstick.

'That's Alec and Bobby Binnie,' one man explained to someone who enquired as to the reason for such enthusiastic applause. 'They're brothers. Alec's the one blowin' the trumpet in the Sally Army Band and that's Bobby knockin' hell out o' that drum with the Commy lot. Alike as two peas in a pod to look at. But different in every other way. They're definitely heading in opposite directions – in more ways than one!'

The man's off-the-cuff, roadside assessment of Alec's and Bobby's separate paths in life was accurate as far as it went. But what he could not know was that the divergence in the roads they had taken in life had come about not, as most of their contemporaries supposed, merely because of their different personalities, but from their contrasting reactions to the dark and terrible shadow that hung over their lives. Finding the answer to the question of how that darkness might be penetrated by a greater light had become their mutual passion. But the answers they had found to that question had set them on seemingly opposite tracks.

From the night almost eight years ago when he'd staggered home with the help of his sons, Sandy Binnie had never again gone looking for work. In fact, he'd rarely left home other than to walk every Friday evening to the pub at the end of the street from which he would return just after closing time and much the worse for wear. Sometimes he would stay in bed for days at a time, hardly speaking more than a brief and grudging sentence or two to his wife and sons. When he did get up, he would sit in the armchair wrapped in a blanket whatever the weather. For a while, the minister from the kirk where he'd attended every week, taught in Sunday school, and served in a variety of youth activities, called on him monthly and sought to counsel and pray with him. But his attempts to minister to his erstwhile church member were met only with a contemptuous shake of the head and an adamant refusal. His old Boys' Brigade colleagues came to see him on a number of occasions encouraging him to resume his previous role and encountered the same angry response. Inevitably, as time went on, their visits grew less frequent until they stopped completely.

A doctor from the local panel, whose fees were paid by an ex-servicemen's charity in the town, came to the house to examine him and diagnosed nothing more specific than 'shell shock'. He could suggest no treatment apart from rest and offer no prospect of improvement other than the hope that 'things might get a little better over time'. The effect on Peggy of watching the bright and energetic man she'd married withdraw into himself and fall prey to dark and angry moods was to age her prematurely. Though only in her mid-thirties, she looked and felt like someone twenty years older. The impact on the boys of watching their father deteriorate and their mother become old before her time was to stir within them a deep sense that all was not well with the world, and a determination to discover whatever was needed to change it. But it was that shared passion that took their lives in opposite directions and led to them marching to the music of two different bands.

Before they'd both left home to get married, Alec in 1924 and Bobby a year later, the brothers would often argue heatedly about the root causes of the injustice that confronted them in the suffering of their father and in the world at large. Initially, they'd both agreed, in common with virtually all their fellow-miners, that the Labour Party, which had gained a firm foothold in working-class communities across Britain, was their natural political home and a powerful force in the fight for a better and fairer world. It was an allegiance that Alec maintained for the rest of his life. But Bobby, who had come under the influence of the much more radical Communist movement, gradually hardened in his conviction that what needed to be changed were the underlying structures of society. The war that had all but robbed them of their father and the poverty they could see all around them were neither inevitable nor accidental. They were the result, Bobby insisted, of an unjust division of wealth and power, an imbalance that was underpinned and reinforced by the long-established institutions of government and the acquiescence of what he saw as a corrupt and compromised Church. Merely striking for better working conditions or negotiating for a fairer weekly wage would amount to little more than tampering around the edges of things. Asking nicely for change, he would often comment to his brother, would achieve nothing because the existing processes of democracy were weighted heavily against any deep and lasting transformation of society. Those in power would never put their own position and status at risk. What was needed was a revolution that would overthrow the existing world order, remove the privileged and wealthy elite from their gilded palaces, and ensure that the working classes would enjoy the benefits of their labours.

Bobby's interest in Communism had been fuelled by the passionate speeches of charismatic agitators whose fiery rhetoric drew crowds of disillusioned men to their meetings in draughty public halls. But the flame of his wholehearted commitment to their fiery brand of Marxist socialism was stoked by long and intense half-whispered conversations with the committed disciples of this anti-capitalist creed who patiently shared their faith with sincere seekers after justice for the masses in the smoke-filled back rooms of Bellmill's pubs. Ironically, his road to conversion was to a great extent the mirror image of his older brother's journey in the opposite direction.

The year before his marriage, Alec was standing at a corner of the crossroads at the centre of the town on a Sunday evening with two acquaintances. 'Bellmill Cross', as it was known by everyone, was a favourite meeting place for young men with plenty of time on their hands and a little money in their pockets. The three young friends had both time and money on that evening and they were intending to slake their thirst in one of the many pubs for which Bellmill was famed, when their curiosity was aroused by the arrival of around twenty uniformed members of the local corps of The Salvation Army which had been established in the town around the turn of the century. Alec and his companions immediately decided to postpone their visit to the Crossroads Inn. This offered the unexpected but welcome prospect of some free amusement at the expense of these 'Hallelujahs', as they were popularly known, whose unusual methods of attracting attention had not only provoked derision from some quarters but had also drawn no little criticism from a number of the more established and respectable churches in the town.

The dozen or so bandsmen took up their instruments and began to accompany the singers, somewhat untunefully in the opinion of several in the audience that quickly gathered. Much to the amusement of Alec and his companions, the song had a recurring refrain that demanded to know if the listeners were 'washed in the blood of the Lamb', a question that gave them ample opportunity to offer a variety of ribald responses. The fact that the objects of their ridicule seemed quite unperturbed quickly took all the fun out of their mockery and they decided it was time to abandon the scene and seek some immediate liquid refreshment. They were on the point of leaving when Alec's attention was caught by one of the uniformed evangelists who looked vaguely familiar and who'd begun addressing the crowd in a voice loud enough to be heard above the traffic. To his surprise, he realised that the speaker was a man he'd worked alongside for a few weeks a year or two back in the Black Moss Colliery. He couldn't recall his name, but he could clearly remember that he was one of the most foul-mouthed and belligerent miners he'd ever met. His pals were bored and impatient to get to the pub. Alec, however, was rooted to the spot, spellbound at what he was seeing and hearing. He was transfixed by the unsophisticated eloquence of a man with the courage to stand at the junction of the main roads through the town and declare to anyone who would listen that he was done with the past and that his life had been transformed for good. He concluded his brief unscripted testimony in two sentences that lodged themselves in Alec's mind.

'I used to think that the world was all wrong and that I'd be a happier man if things were different. The truth is that it was me who was wrong and I was the one who needed to be changed.'

Twenty minutes later, much to his own surprise, Alec had separated from his companions and was sitting on an uncomfortable wooden form on the back row of the Bellmill Salvation Army barracks. He'd followed the band as they'd marched back to their hall for their evening meeting, drawn irresistibly by the uncomplicated but powerful message he'd just heard. It seemed to crystallise what he'd been struggling to understand and articulate in his arguments with his brother. Yes, the world was in a sorry state and needed to be changed. Any sane person could see it. That was why he'd aligned himself with the Labour Party. But the world was what it was because of the people who lived in it, the people who saw things only from their own perspective, the people who put themselves first, the people who found it hard to say sorry for their mistakes and even harder to forgive others for theirs. It was people who needed to be changed if ever the world was to be changed. *People like him*.

At first, the unfamiliar concoction of informality, spontaneity and uninhibited religious fervour was disconcerting to him. Tambourines and hand-clapping and loud shouts of 'Hallelujah' and 'Amen' had never been part of the more sombre and reflective worship of the Church of Scotland in which he'd been raised. But there was an undeniable warmth and sincerity about the proceedings that spoke to him and drew him in as no other experience of worship had ever done.

He went home that night without telling his mother or brother where he'd been and unsure whether he would attend again. But he did go back the following week, and the one after that. And each time he went he felt a little more at home, quickly learning that what he was attending was the 'salvation meeting', a service convened intentionally and unapologetically as an evangelistic gathering and designed always to end with an appeal for sinners to come forward and claim forgiveness for their wrongdoing. On the fourth Sunday evening, when the appeal was made, he got up and, with tears streaming down his face, made his way to the front. He knelt at the 'mercy seat', a wooden bench with the words 'Come unto Me' inscribed along the back, where Frank Simpson, the man he'd heard speaking in the open-air service a month before, knelt beside him and prayed with him.

It was a life-changing moment for Alec. Within two months he'd signed his 'Articles of War' and promised that he would be 'by God's help a true soldier of The Salvation Army till I die'. On the Sunday he was publicly enrolled as a Salvation Army solider, he told the congregation that, just like his father before him, he had enlisted in an army. The difference was, he added to a chorus of hallelujahs and amens, this was the *real* army – one that relied not on the destructive power of guns, but on the transforming power of God.

A year later, he married Irene Moffat. She was eighteen months younger than he was and one of a group of attractive young women who sat in the front row of the choir that he learned to call The Songster Brigade as he quickly mastered the jargon of the group he'd joined. It had been love at first sight and it resulted in a marriage that lasted a lifetime. His mother, who thought it odd that the bride and groom wore their navy-blue uniforms for the marriage ceremony, had to be content with the explanation that it was simply a way of announcing to everyone present that their love for God came before even their love for each other. It was not a distinction that she found easy to understand, but it left her in no doubt that her eldest son had changed. And she was content to accept that the change had been for the better.

chapter 5
fathers and sons
1928–57

Sandy Binnie died at the age of forty-five on the morning of Sunday 11th November 1928 as the nation was observing the tenth anniversary of the signing of the armistice and lauding its fallen and wounded heroes who had fought bravely for king and country. He was still sitting slouched in the armchair by the dying embers of a coal fire with a blanket wrapped round his shoulders when Peggy found him on her return from church. She closed his eyes and gently stroked his white hair that still retained a hint of the sandy colouring that she'd found so attractive when they'd first met. She picked up the half-finished tumbler of whisky lying on the hearthstone beside him and sighed to herself as she held the smooth glass in her cupped hands.

In the earlier years of their marriage – before her husband had returned from France a broken man – she'd adamantly refused to have alcohol in the house. But though she herself never felt the need for anything stronger than 'a nice cup of hot tea', she had abandoned her rigid principle for what she felt was a greater good. It was only after Sandy had drunk a dram or two of Scotch that the thick fog of depression that hung over him shutting him off from the rest of the world would sometimes lift and allow him to engage with his family. And there were even occasional flashes of sunlight – bittersweet moments when he would express an interest in what was going on around him and she would catch a precious glimpse of the man she'd married and missed so much. But the dark clouds would roll back just as quickly as they had parted and he would stumble back into a confused and introspective monologue or lose himself in an impenetrable silence.

The loss of his leg and the discomfort and pain of getting around on the primitive prosthetic limb with which he'd been provided might have been in themselves obstacles that he could have overcome with help and patience. But it was the guilt that never left him – guilt for what he'd seen on the battlefield, guilt at his ineptitude as a soldier, guilt at his own survival while good men had died all around him, guilt at his loss of faith, guilt at his inability to cope – and it became an insurmountable barrier before which he fell helpless and defeated. The doctor who certified his death recorded that it was 'due to natural causes', but he offered no argument when Peggy said that the real cause of death had been a broken heart. Friends and neighbours who called dutifully expressed their condolences at her loss, though they whispered to each other that she had really lost her husband a decade before and that his death must have come as a merciful release from the pain of watching his personality disintegrate as his suffering only increased.

Both his sons spoke at the funeral service. Alec, wearing his Salvation Army uniform, gave thanks for the example he'd been given as a child and expressed his heartfelt desire that his father had made his peace with God and sought the forgiveness that we all need. Our trust when we lose someone we love, he told the congregation, must be firmly set on the infinite love and mercy of God. And our hope should be focused on a resurrection morning when all tears would be wiped away, all things would be made new, and the dead would be raised to eternal life. Bobby's words, in sharp contrast, were less of a eulogy and more of a tirade against the injustice and cruelty of a world that had robbed his father of his health and his dignity; a world which needed fixing, not in some ethereal realm or on some far-off day, but here and now; a world in which war would be consigned to the dustbin of history; a world in which the extremes of wealth and poverty would be replaced by equal opportunities for all and a fair distribution of resources. He ended his impassioned speech by quoting, not from the Bible, but from the poetry of Robert Burns. Though the verse was in the form of a prayer, he was quick to point out that it was a prayer whose fulfilment lay not in the hoped-for intervention of a distant God or in the second coming of a divine saviour, but in the willingness of men and women to roll up their sleeves and fight for change at the first opportunity.

> Then let us pray that come it may,
> (As come it will for a' that,)
> That Sense and Worth, o'er a' the earth,
> Shall bear the gree, an' a' that.

For a' that, an' a' that,
It's coming yet for a' that,
That Man to Man, the world o'er,
Shall brothers be for a' that.

The contrasting manifestos that the brothers presented that day were the closing sentences in what had been a long and exhausting chapter. The family mourned with sincerity the loss of a husband and father who had seen terrible things and suffered more than any man should. But, though none of them would have felt able to admit or even recognise the truth at that moment, his passing had freed them to move on with their lives and follow the paths that his continuing presence would have blocked to them. In a little over twelve months Peggy, despite the raised eyebrows of some of her friends and neighbours who felt it was much too soon to discard her widow's black mourning weeds, had remarried a widower a few years older than she was whom she met while visiting an old friend in Edinburgh. She left Bellmill to live in Scotland's capital city, becoming the wife of a school janitor and stepmother to his three adult children in addition to being mother to her own two sons. It was a long and loving relationship in which she found the happiness that she had thought would never again be hers. Bobby, for whom working underground had always been an ordeal, moved to Glasgow with his wife, found employment in the shipyards, and rose to become a prominent and respected figure in the shipworkers' union. His name was remembered fondly and with great respect by working-class Glaswegians long after he died whenever they recited a roll-call of the heroes of what the popular press called 'Red Clydeside'.

Alec, however, had no desire to live anywhere other than Bellmill or to look for work outside of coalmining.

'What else could I do?' he would ask his mother with an easy laugh whenever she tentatively suggested that he might consider finding employment that carried less of a risk to life and limb. 'It's all I've known since I left school. Anyway, coalmining's a lot less dangerous than what my poor old dad had to go through. And this town's my home. Why would I want to live anywhere else?'

But that wasn't all that kept him living in Bellmill and working at the Black Moss Colliery. *What really mattered was that he had found his vocation right where he was and nothing would distract him from it.* The Salvation Army had become much more to him than merely the church he attended. It had commissioned him as a soldier with a God-ordained assignment in the great cosmic battle of good against evil; it had given him an identity and a dignity as a member of a movement that had once been sneeringly dismissed as 'corybantic Christianity' but was increasingly respected for its practical care and concern for those in need; it had even provided him with a vibrant alternative culture in which the martial music of the brass band and the vivid drama of its simple but colourful ceremonies offered an appealing alternative to the grey drabness of much of life in the first half of the twentieth century. He was a man with a purpose who knew he was in the right place.

As the years passed, there was only one thing missing from life for Alec and Irene Binnie – the thing they wanted more than anything else. They looked at the couples around them with their growing families and longed for children of their own. It was the cause of more than a few tears and a subject for much prayer. After a decade of waiting and hoping and praying, they accepted their childlessness as God's will and Irene threw herself wholeheartedly into teaching in Sunday school and working with young people as a productive way of compensating for what she had been advised was a congenital inability to bear children. But sixteen years after their marriage in 1924, when visiting a doctor about her persistent nausea, she was shocked to be told the reason for how she'd been feeling. At first, she couldn't comprehend the words she was hearing. And then she blushed with embarrassment at her stupidity in not immediately realising the cause of her sickness in the mornings.

'You're not ill, Mrs Binnie, I'm glad to say. You're expecting a baby.'

'Are you... are you sure?' she stammered.

'Well, I must have looked after hundreds of pregnant women in my time,' the doctor replied with a chuckle. 'And you're at least as pregnant as any of them.'

Alec was on *backshift* that day – working from two o'clock in the afternoon until ten at night – so she had to wait until eleven o'clock when he'd finished his supper before she could tell him her news. He was just as dumbfounded as she had been earlier in the day, but his surprise quickly gave way, not to embarrassment, but to elation. He stood up and held her in a long embrace, unable either to speak or to stop the tears trickling down his face. When he did eventually release his hold on her, he made her sit down, telling her she should be resting, while he went to the kitchen and brought the kettle to the boil again. He came back carrying two cups of tea which he set on the table very carefully before sitting down beside her. She thought she'd never seen him look so happy.

'Rene,' he said very deliberately, missing off the first syllable of her name as he always did when he felt he had something of more than usual importance to say to her, 'this is a miracle. A miracle. We'll have to take special care of this child. And we need to take special care of you while you're carrying him. But before anything else, we ought to say thanks…'

And there and then they held hands and bowed their heads as he offered a prayer of gratitude for an unexpected blessing. It was only after his prayer had ended and they were drinking their tea that she thought about his words to her a few moments earlier.

'Did you realise what you said?' she asked. 'You just said, "while you're carrying *him*". But you don't know that it's going to be a boy. I'm sure we'd be just as happy with a little girl.'

'Of course we would,' he responded. 'Especially if she looked like you. But it's just that as soon as you told me… well, I had the feeling it'll be a boy.'

Whether or not Alec's words were the result of some divine revelation or just a lucky guess, neither of them was ever able to say for certain. But what was undeniable was that at precisely five minutes past midnight on Friday 14th March 1941, as Bobby Binnie and his family were fleeing for their lives from the death and destruction being wreaked by the Luftwaffe on Clydeside less than twenty miles away, Alec and Irene Binnie were welcoming their first and only child – a healthy baby boy. They gave him the name Alexander, like his father and grandfather before him, and showered him with love and attention. And on a Sunday morning when their baby was less than a month old, they stood in front of the congregation of the Bellmill Salvation Army, gave thanks for the gift of their child and pledged that they would protect him from anything that might harm him and encourage him to devote his life to the service of God and others.

The food shortages and rationing imposed by the government during the Second World War made raising and providing a child with adequate nutrition a challenge for any family. But, though he was still too young to realise it, the boy was fortunate in having both parents living at home to share in his upbringing and devote themselves to his welfare. Whereas many families had lost the man of the house to the British Army, the government considered the coalmining industry to be essential to the war effort, and consequently its workers were exempt from conscription. Alec's presence throughout the war years was a double blessing of which the Binnies were not unmindful. It meant that he was spared the trials of military life that had so damaged his father and it allowed a powerful emotional bond to be forged between father and son.

By the time the war ended in 1945 the third Alexander Binnie was a sturdy four-year-old with a boundless energy that sometimes left his mother on the point of exhaustion. Everyone, including his parents, knew him as Ecky, a nickname that arose from his early childish efforts to get his tongue round the four tricky syllables of the impressive but unpronounceable name his parents had given him. He was popular with other children and was always at the centre of any group of his peers in which he found himself. From the time he could walk and talk he seemed to have the happy knack of getting along well with everyone. But there was nothing that could compare to or compete with the close relationship he had with his father. He was happy to be in his dad's company at any time, just watching him or waiting for him to finish whatever he was doing. And whenever that point was reached, he would nag him until he gave in to his son's pleadings and they would make their way together to the nearest stretch of grass where they could kick a ball to each other.

Those were the times that Alec began to realise that his young son's fascination with football went beyond the usual interest that the boys around him had in the game. Even at that age, it was obvious to anyone who watched him that he was a natural with a ball at his feet. Irene, whose father had played semi-professionally with a local team in his younger days, insisted that it was a talent he must have inherited from her side of the family. Alec found such pleasure in the lad's company that it never occurred to him to question where his skill with a football had come from. Nor did it ever cross his mind that it might one day become an obsession that would stretch the previously indestructible bond between them to breaking point.

All the time he was at primary school, Ecky Binnie was never a problem to his parents. He was happy at home and fitted comfortably into school life. His teachers described him as bright boy, a popular pupil and a natural leader. The only criticism they would occasionally make of him was that if his interests didn't lie in other directions and if he applied himself to his school work with greater diligence, he had the ability to do significantly better academically. 'More focused on sport than on study' was a phrase that occurred more than once in the school reports he brought home. But such slight disapproval was always tempered by the headmaster's comments that were included at the bottom of the blue card Ecky brought home to his parents at the end of each school year. Mr McArdle had been an athlete of some distinction in his younger days and was proud of the fact that under his watch the school was near the top of the table for most sports in county competitions. And he was well aware of Ecky's prowess at games. 'Good in the classroom and outstanding on the football field. Well done!' or some similar form of words always summed up his positive opinion of his star footballer's contribution to the school.

What mattered just as much to his father was that Ecky fitted happily into the life and activities of The Salvation Army. As an eager seven-year-old he had responded one Sunday morning, along with another four children of his age, to the invitation to 'give his heart to Jesus'. He wasn't entirely sure how that worked and what it would involve, but he knew it was the right thing to do and he knew his dad would be pleased. A month or two later he signed his promise card, pledging himself to live a life that was 'clean in thought, word and deed' and, watched by his moist-eyed parents, he was sworn in as a Junior Soldier.

That phrase *sworn in* confused him as they'd been solemnly warned more than once in Sunday school that boys who swore were committing a really bad sin. But he decided that grown-ups must have a reason for using those words, a reason that would be too complicated for young people of his age to understand. He'd wait until he was older before asking for an explanation. And, anyhow, it didn't seem nearly as important or interesting as playing football. Before another year passed, he learned to play his first tune on the cornet and joined the junior band. He enjoyed being part of the group of youthful musicians, but he did find it difficult to sit still through the often fiery sermons and lengthy prayer sessions of the three services that his parents expected him to attend with them every Sunday. He did, however, become adept at diverting his attention and devising ways of keeping himself occupied. The competition with the other boys to see who could be the first to count all the knots in the wood panelling on the wall in front of them kept them occupied and quiet through many a long Sunday evening.

And so things might have continued, but for two things that changed: Ecky Binnie began to develop from a child into a youth with an independent personality, and he transferred to secondary school. There was one thing, however, that didn't change: football remained his first love and abiding passion. Although he wasn't quite thirteen, the enthusiastic gym teacher who was responsible for the school first eleven spotted his talent and immediately chose him for the team. His ability to outplay older boys who stood head and shoulders above him quickly made him a hero among his fellow-pupils for whom prowess on the football field trumped academic attainment any day. For the next three years, he was the undisputed star player. Inevitably his displays began to attract the attention of the scouts who were employed to look out for boys who might have the potential to play the game professionally. And most of those scouts had the name of the stocky youngster with the shock of wavy, sandy-coloured hair pencilled in their notebooks.

That was when things began to go wrong between father and son. There were not many months when someone representing one or other of the teams playing in Scotland's Division One didn't knock on the door of the Binnie family holding out the prospect of a career in professional football. Ecky was excited at the possibility and eager to accept their invitation to take part in a trial. His father, however, was deeply troubled at the thought of his son following such a path in life. For a start, it was an uncertain business, he would tell him. Career-ending injuries could happen at any time. Playing football for fun was one thing. Earning your living from the game was altogether different. And, what was even more important, it was a morally questionable profession in his father's eyes. People actually paid money to stand and watch football matches. That made it a form of – the words were spoken in the tone of voice that someone might use when speaking of a deadly virus – *worldly entertainment,* something that no good Salvationist could countenance. Ecky would be separating himself from the way of life in which he had been raised and involving himself with people to whom religion meant little or nothing and for whom the name of Jesus Christ was a mere profanity.

The boy listened to the arguments being put to him by his father with growing frustration. Little by little the tensions between them grew until what had started as conversations degenerated into heated arguments and finally gave way to the pent-up irritation of a middle-aged man and the sullen silence of a sixteen-year-old youth. The breaking point came when Ecky, without his father's prior knowledge or permission, accepted the invitation to take part in a trial with one of the Edinburgh teams that had been arranged for a Sunday morning. His parents woke to find that he would not be playing his cornet in the band that day. He'd already gone, leaving a note informing them in just a couple of brief sentences where he was going and what he'd be doing that day. It was a message that would have long-lasting consequences for life in the Binnie family.

chapter 6
different goals
1959–84

A year after signing professional forms, Ecky Binnie
proudly pulled on the maroon jersey of the 'Castles',
Edinburgh's biggest and best-supported team, for the first
time. It was Saturday 14th March 1959 and it was his
eighteenth birthday. The crowd immediately warmed to
the short but muscular young centre forward whose
scoring exploits for the reserves had been attracting
attention and bringing calls for his promotion to the first
eleven for months. Their expectations were fulfilled when
he scored the only goal of the game with a low rasping
shot just before the referee blew the whistle for full-time.
And it wasn't only the Castle supporters who were excited
about the debutant.

'What Binnie lacks in height,' the football
correspondent of the Sunday newspaper observed, 'he
more than makes up for in his ability to run at the
opposition and his refusal to be knocked off the ball by
defenders who are half a foot or more taller than he is. This
young man is definitely one to watch.'

He was still in bed when his doting landlady brought the paper to his bedroom with a cup of tea before she left for church. More than thirty years after the death of her first husband, Sandy, Peggy McPhee, as she'd become, still sprightly though in her eighties, had been widowed for a second time. The house felt too big and empty now that she was on her own again. When she learned that relationships had become strained between her son Alec and her grandson back in her home town and that Ecky was coming to Edinburgh to pursue a career in football, she was eager to have him as her lodger. It'd be good company for her and she could keep an eye on him. Make sure he didn't stray too far from the straight-and-narrow. She might even be able to encourage him to keep a link with his parents. And she was pretty sure that, for his part, Ecky would raise no objections to having his grandmother fuss over him and tend to his every need.

'If I'd known you'd become this famous,' she said, waving the newspaper lauding her grandson's performance the previous afternoon, 'I'd have doubled your rent. So don't go getting above yourself just because your name's in the paper, or I might just do that.'

She laughed as she put the cup on the bedside table and threw the paper onto his bed.

'There. You can read all about yourself while I'm gone and I'll make a spot of lunch when I get back.'

Peggy was a regular at St Andrew's kirk on a Sunday morning. But her brand of religion was a little more reserved, a good deal more liberal and easy-going, and considerably less proselytising than that of her son. All of which suited Ecky's current attitude towards matters of faith. In addition, she had that instinctive understanding that grandparents often have of how to relate to their own children's offspring.

'He's not a bad boy,' she'd told Alec when she'd met up with him in a café on Edinburgh's Princes Street to tell him that she was going to offer Ecky lodgings at her home. 'But he's young and he wants to play football more than anything else. You've got to let him do what he wants to do. If we try to stop him doing that, he could end up resenting us for the rest of his life. Trust me. I'll make sure he's OK.'

And that's just what she did for more than two years until he was earning enough to allow him to move out and rent a flat near the Castle Stadium. She was sorry to see him go, but she knew that it was the right time for him to make his own way in life. She consoled herself in the knowledge that she'd done a good job. Though she'd had no success in effecting any kind of reconciliation between father and son, she had been able to offer her homespun, grandmotherly counsel at what she sensed were the appropriate moments without provoking the resentment he might well have felt in a more direct confrontation with his parents.

All the while his career had been progressing steadily. His name was one of the first on the Castle's team sheet every week and his place as a favourite of the fans was firmly established. It was no surprise to those who knew the game well and followed his progress closely that Ecky Binnie was being mentioned with increasing regularity whenever the selectors met in Glasgow to choose a team to represent Scotland in their annual spring clashes with the 'Auld Enemy'. The two great rivals were due to face each other at Hampden Park on 15th April 1961, just a month after his twenty-first birthday. It was, the newspapers were saying, the perfect time for a young man who was now reaching maturity as a footballer to be given his first call-up to the national team. He tried hard not to get carried away by all the speculation, but it was impossible for him not to be excited at the prospect of donning the dark-blue shirt and walking on to the hallowed turf of the national stadium to the sound of the famous 'Hampden Roar'.

On Saturday 1st April, two weeks before the international match and a few days before the Scottish team to play against England would be announced to the public, the Castles were playing against their local rivals from the other side of the city. As always in such derby matches, the atmosphere was tense and the game was being played at a frenetic pace. The referee was doing his best to keep the emotions of the twenty-two men on the field in check, blowing his whistle frequently, and warning them that he wouldn't hesitate to send someone off if there was one more example of the kind of aggressive challenge that could result in serious injury to an opposing player.

For the first half hour Ecky had been on the periphery of the action, unable to make any impression on the hard-tackling defenders he was facing. Suddenly he had the ball at his feet and a gap opened up in front of him, leaving him with a clear run-in on goal. It was the moment he'd been waiting for. That one golden opportunity that had to be taken. He could see the goalkeeper coming towards him and he knew he had to shoot. Just as he swung back his right leg ready to strike the ball, he caught a glimpse out of the corner of his eye of someone lunging towards him from the side, both feet off the ground, in a last-ditch effort to halt his progress. There was no time to take any evasive action. He heard a sharp crack. A sound he'd never heard before. It was immediately followed by a searing pain, worse than anything he'd ever felt. His body seemed to crumple beneath him and he skidded along the turf. A wave of nausea and dizziness swept over him. He couldn't work out exactly what had happened until he looked down at his leg. It was a strange shape. It shouldn't be that shape! Then he saw the concerned faces of his teammates looking down at him. And, in a flash, the awful truth dawned on him. The thing that every footballer dreaded. His leg was broken.

The boos from the terraces as his assailant was ordered from the pitch gave way to a concerned silence as he was gently lifted on to a stretcher, and then to sympathetic applause as he was carried off the field. The supporters who'd been singing his name a few minutes before knew that this was a serious injury and a significant setback in the career of one of their heroes. Ecky Binnie would certainly not be taking the field against the English in two weeks' time and it would be many months before they would see him with a ball at his feet again.

In fact, it would be a year and a half before he would be back in action. When he did return, they welcomed him with enthusiastic cheers and high hopes. But it was obvious after the first few matches that he was not the player he had been. The sudden turn of speed that had left opposing defenders in his wake, the instinctive predatory touch in front of goal, the hint of arrogance that great players need – they had all deserted him. The more optimistic among the supporters put it down to the 'rustiness' that was only to be expected after such a long lay-off. Give him time and he'll be back to his old self before too long, they predicted. But time in this case was not the great healer.

At the end of the following season he was placed on the transfer list and was signed by an English Second Division team. It was the beginning of a decade-long traipse through some of English and Scottish football's remoter outposts as he dropped down the leagues, eking out a living in the only profession he knew. There were occasional flashes of the brilliance of his earlier years, but they served only to remind those on the sparsely populated terraces who now watched him of what he had once been. At twenty-one he'd been considered one of the brightest prospects of his generation and his goal had been to represent his country and leave an indelible mark on the sport he loved. At thirty-one he was described by one sports' reporter as 'a faded star, a journeyman player who doesn't usually last longer than one season at any club'. Now his goal was just to survive as long as he could in the game before the lingering effect of his career-transforming injury and the ravages of time forced him to look for regular employment outside the sport that had once promised him so much.

In the course of his decline as a footballer, despite repeated efforts from his parents and grandmother to repair the rift, he became increasingly isolated from his family, refusing to meet with them or even respond to their phone calls and letters. His anger at his father's initial unhappiness at his choice of career was compounded by a deeper rage at having been prevented from reaching his potential as a footballer. Whether it was fate, or sheer bad luck, or the malevolent will of the god his father believed in, he neither knew nor cared. What he did know for sure was that he was living in a world where life seldom went to plan, where people got hurt, and where hopes could be cruelly dashed in the blink of an eye.

He played his last game as a professional footballer in May 1972. By that time, he was living in a flat just off the Holloway Road in north London with a woman called Sue Ramsey and their seven-month-old baby boy. They'd met two years earlier when she was working as a part-time secretary in the office of the football club he was playing for at that time. He was fed up living in digs and she was just coming out of an abusive marriage. They gravitated towards each other out of loneliness and the need for human comfort.

They'd barely had time to get to know each other properly before they moved in together, and within a few months she'd fallen pregnant. At first there were frequent heated arguments between them, and the few people who were close enough to them to be aware of the situation assumed that this was yet another relationship was that was doomed to fail. Against all the odds, however, and for reasons neither of them could readily explain to anyone else, what had been a hasty and ill-considered liaison slowly became, with the passage of the years, a permanent and settled state. Initially, their relationship did not run smoothly. Nor was their home, especially in the early days, a haven of unbroken domestic bliss. Their cohabitation had neither the legal status of marriage nor the sanction and blessing of the Church until they'd been together for more than thirty years. But they were bound by a mutual recognition that life had brought them together and a dogged determination to make the best of things. It wasn't the stuff of romantic fiction. It was, however, a down-to-earth view of life that proved strong enough to withstand the strain of passing attractions and to hold firm until they were parted by death.

It was only after he'd hung up his boots for the last time that Ecky realised how physically and emotionally exhausted he was. The end of his footballing career, though it was heavy with the bitter aftertaste of disappointment at what might have been, came as a relief. At least it afforded him an escape from the relentless treadmill of training throughout the week, driving his body through one injury after another, and pushing himself to compete for ninety minutes every Saturday. The further he dropped down the football pyramid, the rougher the treatment he received from opposing players, hardened professionals who were less talented than he was, but all the more determined to employ whatever dirty tricks were needed to stop him in his tracks. And the longer it went on, the greater the effort that was required to push himself to his limit week after week for diminishing returns on the football pitch.

For months after his retirement from the game, he felt lost in a fog of weariness and apathy through which he caught glimpses of other people getting on with things that made up normal life, things that he'd never been free to do as an adult. It took him until the winter of 1972 before he summoned up sufficient energy to give some thought as to what he might do with the rest of his life and how he might earn a living. On yet another morning when he couldn't be bothered to get out of bed, Sue, who'd been up for some time looking after their child, came into the bedroom and threw a copy of the newspaper at him. It was open at the page with the job adverts, one of which she'd circled in black ink.

'Pomphrey's Funeral Directors on the Holloway Road are looking for men who want to start a second career.' There was a sarcastic edge to her voice and she had the expression of someone who was on the point of running out of patience. 'The money looks decent. You should apply. You've got a miserable look on your face all the time. I think you'd fit perfectly into that line of work.'

He was about to turn over and bury his head under the blankets when he had a sense of déjà vu. *This had happened to him before.* Thirteen years before, to be exact. At a very different moment in his life a different woman had thrown a different newspaper open at a different page on to the bed for him to read. But he was a different man from that carefree and starry-eyed young footballer living in his grandmother's spare room. And yet... *He was still Ecky Binnie.* He still had years to live. He still had to earn a living. He still had to do something with his life. The last time this had happened he'd sat up and read the paper. There was no reason why he shouldn't sit up and read it now.

That was it. He never could work out what made him sit up in bed and pick up the newspaper. Or why he decided to read the job ad that Sue had circled for him. Or why he got up, got dressed, and walked to Pomphrey's Funeral Directors. *But he did.* He went back twice more. And after three interviews they offered him a job.

In his mind it was only temporary, just to tide him over until something more suitable turned up. But, to his surprise, the work suited him. The pain of the past slowly numbed. There was even a measure of healing, emotionally as well as physically, and gradually he began to feel alive again. Bruised and battered by life, undeniably. But alive. Being an undertaker answered a deep need that he'd never understood or even known was there. Once he'd thought that the adulation of an adoring crowd might fill his need for significance. Now he discovered that the heartfelt thanks of a bereaved family satisfied it in a way that the cheers of partisan supporters never had. He was actually doing something worthwhile. He was *somebody* worthwhile.

He stayed with Pomphrey's Funeral Directors, finding a niche, developing hitherto undreamed-of skills, and making himself generally indispensable to the smooth running of the business. Twelve years after beginning what he thought was a *pro tem* job, he bought the business when old Mr Pomphrey retired. He never spoke about or even gave much thought to his previous career. But he did allow himself a wry smile when one of his first tasks on taking over the company was to approve the slogan on the cover of a new brochure publicising the company's services. It read simply: *Our goal is to help you say goodbye with grace and dignity*. He sat back in his chair with his hands behind his head and looked up at the ceiling. If only he'd been able to do that when he'd walked off the football pitch for the last time...

chapter 7
family affairs
1989

That's my family history. It's not the whole story, of course. Like most history it's only what the author considers to be the key moments in the tale that they have to tell. And there's so much that I haven't touched on. So much that I don't know. So much – all the minutiae of daily existence that makes up the greater part of our lives – that there's never time or space to tell. But I've focused on those life-changing episodes, those encounters with triumph and adversity that shape a person's character and set the direction for all that follows. And there's little about the women in my telling of this tale, though even the little I have related should be enough to show that they've been the ones who've held the family together over three generations. Someone should write their story. Write it from the women's point of view, assigning the men to play the bit parts and fade into the background. But my time is short. It's the men I had to tell you about: who they were and why they did what they did. And now I need to begin to tell you *my* story. How my past grows out of their past. How they are part of me and I'm part of them. And, significantly, that link only really began to become clear to me on the day I first began to learn *their* story.

It was just after ten o'clock on Saturday 30th September 1989 when the doorbell rang. I remember the date and time because I was due to leave a couple of hours later to catch a train to Oxford. My mother was in my bedroom with me trying to make sure that I'd packed everything I'd need for my first term at university and my father was downstairs in the kitchen, drinking a second cup of coffee and reading the newspapers at the kitchen table.

'Sue, can you answer that?' he shouted with more than a trace of annoyance in his voice. 'I'm back in the office this afternoon and I'd just like to finish my coffee in peace.'

My mother, equally irritated by this interruption to her attempts to get her only child out of the house with everything he'd need to survive on his own, went grudgingly to the door. The conversation on the doorstep seemed to take considerably longer than those she normally had with unexpected callers who could be courteously but swiftly dismissed. Eventually, however, I heard her say, 'I think you'd better come in.'

I went to the top of the stairs to see who these visitors could be who'd cut short the preparations for my imminent departure. I was just in time to catch sight of an elderly couple being led into the front room before my mother hurried to the kitchen for a brief and whispered exchange of words with my father. His Saturday mornings were sacred to him and always carefully guarded. So, when the kitchen door opened again and he followed my mother into the front room, I guessed that whoever these people were, they must be more important than mere

85

casual callers seeking his attention. There was an expression on his face that I'd never seen before – something between shock and regret and anticipation. I stood still for a few minutes, uncertain what I should do. Then, overcome by curiosity, I tiptoed quietly downstairs and stood by the door to listen.

The elderly man was speaking with what was unmistakably a Scottish accent. There was a slight wheeze in his breathing as he talked, and occasionally he would have to catch his breath.

'I know, son. You've told me before that you didn't want to be in touch. But your mum and me, we're not getting any younger. We're well into our eighties now. Who knows how much longer we'll be around? We didn't want to go to our grave without seeing you face to face... without saying sorry for our part – for my part – in causing the rift between us...'

Whenever I'd asked my father about his past, it had always been a firmly closed book. If I questioned him about his family, he would insist that there was nothing to talk about. He had a series of metaphors ready to block any approach I tried: doors had closed, bridges had been burned, ties had been severed long ago. I knew he was Scottish, of course, though his accent had modified and softened over the years. And I knew he'd played football for some years, though on the few occasions he'd spoken about it he did so in such low-key terms that I assumed it had been only a brief and insignificant part of his life. And I was not persistent in my probing. As young people often tend to do, I dismissed my parents as uninteresting people who'd lived boring lives. But now a window had opened into the past. Here, in our front room, was an elderly man calling my father his *son*. And my father didn't seem to be denying the relationship. The grandparents I'd never known had just turned up! Without thinking about what I was doing, I pushed open the door and demanded to know what was going on.

For a moment no one spoke. It was my father who broke the silence. But rather than answering my question, he turned and addressed the elderly couple.

'This is our son, Alexander. His mother insists on giving him his proper name at home. Says she doesn't want another Ecky in the family. But I think his pals call him Alex.'

His eyes were moist and there was a catch in his voice. I'd never seen him like this. He'd often told me that what made him a good undertaker was his ability to sympathise with people without ever allowing himself to get personally involved. Whether it was intentional on his part or not, it was an emotional detachment he'd carried into his family life. He tried to compose himself before he spoke again. This time he directed his words to me.

'Son, these are your grandparents – my parents, Alec and Irene Binnie. We haven't seen each other for nearly thirty years. And that's been mostly my fault, I'm ashamed to say. They've given up waiting for me to make a move towards them. So they've come down from Scotland to see us.'

The elderly man who'd been holding his wife's hand since I'd walked into the room stood up and came towards me. Despite being a little stooped with age, he was still a good three or four inches taller than my father. One look at his face, however, left no room for any doubt that these men were bound by ties of blood. The prominent chin and firm mouth that people often noticed in Ecky Binnie had obviously been inherited from the man now standing in front of me with a tear trickling down his cheek. I reached out to shake his hand, but he pushed my arm aside, pulled me towards him and held me in a tight embrace.

'Alexander Binnie,' he said, stretching out each word and carefully sounding out every syllable. 'Alexander Binnie. My grandson. I never thought I'd live to see this day. I didn't even know you existed until a minute ago.'

He laughed, and cried, and laughed again. And, by the time he'd released me from his hold, the others in the room were crying or laughing with him, or doing both at the same time.

For the next hour, while my mother served a surprisingly elaborate lunch, I sat between my grandparents on the settee, one holding my right hand and the other my left, and both gripping so tightly that I thought they'd never let go. Stories of a family of which I knew nothing, tales from long before I was born, tumbled out to the same accompaniment of tears and laughter that had filled the room since the arrival of these unexpected visitors. As I listened, I began to have a broader perspective on my life. I wasn't just the son of Ecky and Sue. I was part of a family that stretched back into a past about which I had been unaware, the product of the generations who'd preceded me. And for the first time I was forced to give thought to how people find answers in their search to find meaning in the world and purpose for their lives.

As an undertaker, my father, who so far as I'd been able to judge had no particular religious convictions of his own, had learned to adopt a detached tolerance and a professional respect for the beliefs and practices of all religious faiths. It was a perspective that he carried into our life as a family and that I'd taken for granted since I was old enough to be aware of such matters. Religion was a generally harmless, if somewhat odd, pursuit in which other people found some kind of comfort. But not our family. And now I was hearing a conversation that opened a window on a view of religion that I'd never encountered before. I was sitting between two people – *his parents* – who were not only active Christians, but who still belonged to a denomination whose members were so committed in their beliefs that they were willing to parade in military-style uniforms as a public display of their faith. A denomination to which my father himself had once belonged!

Then there was his previous life as a footballer. I could never have guessed that the thick-set man who now comforted the bereaved at burials and cremations, the serious-looking and respectable undertaker, had plied a very different trade in his younger days. That his passion for the game had separated him from his family for so many years. That he'd played with such skill that he'd been on the verge of representing his country until his youthful ambitions had been so cruelly dashed. There was so much about him that I'd never known, never been interested enough to find out. It left me with a jumble of contradicting thoughts and emotions that continue to exercise my mind. I am part of this family: forever included in its ongoing story, yet forever separated from most of it by time and place and circumstance; unaware, until the unexpected arrival of my grandparents, of many of the characters who've made up its cast and most of the events that have formed its plot, yet bound to those characters and those events by ties that can never be completely severed.

We spent so long in the company of my grandparents that I missed my train, and my mother had to drive me to Oxford, leaving my father still talking with our guests. She, of course, had known the broad outline of his life before they met and got together in 1970. But he'd never been willing to offer too many details, beyond saying that his relationship with his parents had broken down irreparably. She'd never met his parents until that morning, and much of what had come out in their conversation was news to her.

We drove through busy traffic for the first half hour of the journey without speaking, both of us trying to take in all that had happened since the ringing of the doorbell had interrupted our last-minute packing. When we reached the outskirts of London and began to make faster progress, I asked her if the unexpected arrival of Alec and Irene Binnie and the revelations that had come from the morning's conversation had upset her in any way.

'No, it didn't upset me,' she said glancing at me and smiling. 'I was a bit emotional, of course. But not upset.'

She thought for a few seconds before going further.

'Your dad and me have been good for each other. We were both in a bit of a mess when we met. I never knew who my father was. And my mother abandoned me when I was just about old enough to start school. I spent my childhood in and out of children's homes. And, by the time I met Ecky Binnie, I was just coming out of one more abusive relationship. I was in a mess and he was the first man who was nice to me. He was at a low point too, trying to come to terms with the fact that his days as a football player were coming to an end. Somehow or other, we managed to prop each other up long enough for both of us to learn how to walk again.'

My mother has always been a slightly nervous driver who keeps her eyes fixed on the road ahead and grips the steering wheel so tightly that we often tease her, telling her that her knuckles have gone white. But now, to my amazement, she glanced quickly across at me, stretched out her left hand, and tousled my hair.

'Folk thought that we'd moved in together way too soon, that we hardly knew each other. And they were probably right. We had some rocky moments when we both wondered if it would last. But then we had you and that made all the difference. You gave us something to work together for. Something that took our attention off ourselves. Dad was really very proud of you. He *is* very proud of you.'

'You're kidding me!' I butted in before she could go any further. 'He's always telling me that I'm wasting my time on all this writing nonsense and I need to be thinking of a proper job. "A reliable profession", as he always describes it in his best undertaker voice.'

She pulled off the road into a convenient lay-by. I could see that she wanted to tell me something important. Too important to be said while driving.

'He's a man. And he's Scottish, for goodness' sake. He's not good at showing his emotions. He's just concerned for you. Worried about you risking everything on a career where the prospects of succeeding are so remote. It's hard for you to understand his disappointment at the way his broken leg put paid to his hopes of being a top-flight footballer. He's found a job that's given him a sense of dignity and worth. But even all these years later, that fear of what life can do to you if you try to fly too high – that's never all that far from his mind.'

I thought she was about to drive off again. But she turned the engine off and swivelled in her seat until she was looking into my face. I'd never seen her looking quite so pleased with herself as she was at that moment.

'And there's something else you need to know. But don't tell your father. I'll tell him myself when the time is right.'

I'd never thought of my mother as cunning or devious in any way. But sitting in the car by the side of the A40 gave me a new appreciation of her conspiratorial skills. Alec and Irene Binnie hadn't turned up at our door that morning by chance. Nor had they taken the initiative in deciding to travel from Scotland in the hope of finding their son and effecting a reconciliation. My mother had set the whole thing up. She'd managed to find out their address, contacted them, sorted out the details of their travel to London, arranged for them to stay in a nearby hotel the previous evening, and feigned surprise with all the confidence of an accomplished actor when they'd rung the doorbell in the morning.

'I knew that deep down your dad really wanted to sort things out,' she said quietly, smiling as she filled me in on her subterfuge. 'He never spoke much about it to me, but on the few occasions I broached the subject of his relationship with your grandparents, I could tell it was troubling him. And I knew he'd never make the first move. A mixture of guilt and embarrassment, I suspect. And maybe, most of all, that old fear of setting his hopes too high and having to deal with disappointment all over again. I thought today was the right time. He'd be at home and, although he'd try not to show his emotions, he'd be a bit tender at your going off to university. I hoped that might make him think a bit more about their feelings at losing him all those years ago. And I knew we'd be able to leave the three of them alone with each other for another hour or so before your dad has to go into Pomphrey's. I can't tell you how relieved I am that my plans worked out so well.'

The rest of the journey passed without either of us saying much more as I tried to digest what I'd just heard and my mother concentrated on negotiating her way through the centre of Oxford. We reached the High Street late in the afternoon where we unloaded the car and carried my belongings up to the accommodation I'd be sharing with two other students. My mother stayed just long enough to make sure that I was settled in before she gave me a quick peck on the cheek and hurried off, reminding me with a wink to behave myself and not to bring disgrace on the family. I stood at the window, watching her as she drove off, and musing over the implications of what she'd told me. It was the first time I'd been confronted with a truth that I would encounter more than once in my life. In a world where the men have always appeared to hold the power and get to play the starring roles, it's often the women who possess the insight to understand what's really happening and the imagination to devise the strategies that will change the course of events.

chapter 8
not in the harmony of things
1989–90

Byron Abercrombie-Brydges was once my best friend, though I knew him for less than a year. I first saw him sauntering towards me through the echoey cloisters of my college, humming to himself and swinging his arms in time to a tune that I didn't recognise and which I suspected he was making up as he went along. He was, I would discover, the kind of person who went through life making it up as he went along.

It was nine o'clock on my second evening at university, and I was feeling out of my depth and at a loss to know what to do with myself. I certainly wasn't prepared for the sight that greeted me as he drew close enough for me to see him more clearly.

I guessed that he must be a year or two older than me, though there was something ageless about his appearance that made it difficult to be sure. His eyes seemed to dart constantly in every direction as if he was looking for something he'd mislaid and couldn't quite remember what it looked like or where he might have left it. There was a preternatural brightness about his pale skin that gave him the aura of an angelic visitor from some heavenly realm for whom this world would be a temporary abode. His shoulder-length, flaxen hair hung loose about his face and moved in the gentle breeze that blew through the quadrangle. His clothing was just as striking as his physical appearance. He was wearing a crumpled fawn-coloured linen suit, a white shirt with cuffs that hung unbuttoned and loose below the sleeves of his jacket, a black and red paisley patterned cravat with a matching silk handkerchief in his breast pocket, expensive handmade brown leather shoes on his feet and, pushed to the back of his head, a light grey high-crowned fedora reminiscent of the type you might see in an American gangster movie set in the era of prohibition. My faux-leather biker-jacket, cheap white T-shirt and faded jeans seemed ordinary and unimaginative in comparison. I could tell immediately that we came from opposite ends of the social spectrum and assumed we would pass each other without speaking or with a cursory nod of the head at the most. To my surprise, he stopped, thrust out his hand, and hailed me like a long-lost friend.

'I'm Byron Howard John Abercrombie-Brydges. But no need for that mouthful when you greet me. Feel free just to call me Byron. All my friends do.'

He delivered this grandiose salutation in a plummy accent that left me in no doubt that he'd come up to Oxford from a school very unlike the north London comprehensive at which I'd been educated.

'And you must be Alexander Binnie. I've been looking for you. I'm in the room on the opposite side of the landing to you, and we're both doing English Lit. Didn't get here until this morning, so couldn't say hello sooner. One of the dons is a friend of my pater. Off the record, he told me a bit about you. Said that one of the things that impressed them in your application was that you're a budding writer. Told me I might find you here. Suggested you'd be an interesting companion.'

He released my hand and I tried without success to think of an adequate response to his enthusiastic greeting. In the end I settled for, 'Nice to meet you too, Byron.'

My faltering monosyllabic response did nothing to hinder the rapid progress of our friendship. Within minutes, he'd draped his arm round my shoulders and was leading me to a wine bar he'd already discovered and whose wares he'd sampled earlier in the evening. It was filled with people with accents like his, people who'd come up to Oxford from expensive public schools. I was definitely out of my comfort zone. My previous experience of alcohol had been limited to a half-pint with my father in the pub at the end of our street on my eighteenth birthday, a rite of passage that had been accompanied by his solemn warnings on the dangers of drinking to excess. This place was much more sophisticated than our local pub, an alien culture of which I had no previous experience. My new-found friend, however, was entirely at home in this setting and made it his business to put me at my ease, introducing me to anyone who'd listen as his 'new best friend'. With his flamboyant mode of dress and laid-back, confident manner, he quickly became the centre of attention, a role he appeared to relish and played with no little panache. It was, to say the least, an interesting experience.

When I was back in my room that night, however, I reconciled myself to the fact that what had been an eye-opening introduction to a slice of student life that was new to me would surely turn out to be a one-off event. An entertaining evening in the company of a colourful character who, I was sure, would gravitate to his own social class as soon as the Michaelmas term got properly under way. The loud knocking and shouting outside my door the following morning made it clear that I had misjudged the character of the student who occupied the room opposite mine.

'Come on, Binnie. Get up. I'm hungry and you must be too. Breakfast's on me.'

I dragged myself out of bed, still the worse for wear from the after-effects of too many glasses of red wine the night before, got dressed quickly and followed Byron Abercrombie-Brydges to the café on the opposite side of the High Street. Just as he'd done in the crowded wine bar on the previous evening, he immediately took centre stage, regaling both staff and customers with his opinion on everything from national politics to the latest shows on the London stage. His idiosyncratic views on every aspect of life, delivered with such authority, might have annoyed his audience if offered by anyone else. But he delivered them with such wit and humour that they provoked only laughter and even brought a round of applause at one point. It was only after we'd finished breakfast, though he'd left most of his uneaten, and the other diners had left to get on with their day, that he stopped performing. He drew his chair closer to the table, spoke more quietly, and became serious.

'Binnie, old chap, here's the thing. I went to the kind of school where they give you a good grounding in English literature and they know how to tutor you for the

Oxbridge entrance exams. Both my parents are alumni of this university and I know how to play the academic game. If I make it to the end of the course and I don't mess up, I'll graduate at the end of three years with a good upper second at least. But I don't really care about that. *Truth is, I want to be a writer.'*

His eyes had flitted incessantly around the room when he'd been entertaining an audience half an hour earlier. Now they became very still and focused. He looked directly at me as he elaborated on his statement.

'I really do want to be a writer. I don't want just to write essays about other writers. I want to *write*. And I don't think I can do it without some help. I can help you negotiate your way through university life. Introduce you to people, teach you the tricks of academic success – all that stuff. But I need you to help me with the writing thing. So what about it? Are you up for it?'

For a moment I wondered if he was joking. Was this just another of his performances, only this time aimed at an audience of one? But he was in deadly earnest. He really meant what he said. Not for the first or last time in his company I found myself struggling to make the right response to his comments.

'Yeah… I guess. But I'm no expert. I've had nothing published yet. I'm still trying to work out who I am and what I want to say. And how to say it!'

'Yes!' he shouted, standing up and reverting to his extrovert persona. 'I knew you'd agree. We'll learn to be writers together. And we can do all the other stuff that writers get to do… You know, parties and late nights and drinking. You won't regret this. I promise you.'

That was it. The friendship was sealed and the deal was done there and then. And so began the closest friendship and the most exhilarating period of my life. It was destined to be short and to end in excruciating pain from which I will never be completely healed however long I live. But while it lasted it was wonderful. There were nights we sat up until dawn, writing feverishly, reading aloud what we'd written to one another, critiquing one another's work. And there were nights when we read from the greats of English literature – the dramatists, the novelists, the poets we aspired to be like one day. But most of all, at his insistence, we devoured the poems of his namesake and hero, Lord Byron. We read his favourite, *Childe Harold's Pilgrimage*, in one go, pausing only occasionally to top up our glasses of wine. It wasn't greatly to my taste and I couldn't understand why this very long, gloomy semi-autobiographical poem following the progress of a disillusioned, world-weary traveller in his journey across Europe on a search for meaning appealed to someone as seemingly hedonistic as my companion. But my protests were always met with the same words: 'You'll understand one day, Binnie.'

And there were other nights. Nights when we did 'all the other stuff that writers get to do'. Nights when I was introduced to hitherto unimagined pleasures. Nights that would leave me with a very unpleasant headache and a slightly uneasy conscience when I woke in the middle of the following day.

By the beginning of the Hilary term in January of the following year, 'Byron and Binnie' had become something of a double act in student circles with an open invitation to all the best parties. Our unexpected celebrity gave scope for our different abilities to emerge. Byron went on developing his gift of entertaining the crowd and holding court wherever we went. I was always happy to stand back, add a few intelligent-sounding comments, and lead the applause from the appreciative audience. For my part I discovered a hitherto unsuspected flair. At school I'd always been viewed as bookish and nerdy. I'd carved out a role for myself by writing material that would amuse my peers, but I was never one of the 'in crowd'. And I'd certainly never thought of myself as being particularly attractive to the opposite sex. Never confident enough to chat up the attractive girls. In this world, however, I didn't need to take the initiative. Having pretentions to literary talent simply added to the charisma that came from standing alongside the eccentric, flamboyant Byron. Binnie became the thoughtful member of the duo, handsome in the way female students imagined a romantic poet might have looked. It was a role I played with all the eagerness of a convert who'd joined an exclusive cult. And it was one that Byron was happy to leave entirely to me.

'There's no competition for the girls,' he'd always say when I'd offer a half-hearted apology the next day for disappearing halfway through the party. 'I'm happy to give you a free rein in that area. I'll be content with another drink and the chance to work the room. You enjoy yourself while you can.'

There were, however, occasional and troubling interruptions to our hedonistic lifestyle. From time to time, Byron would go missing without any prior warning or explanation, locking himself in his room. Sometimes he wouldn't reappear for a couple of days. When I did manage to get him to open the door, he would be listless and unable even to feign any interest in life. But then the dark depression would lift as suddenly as it had descended on him. He'd emerge from his room with an even more colourful outfit as if nothing had happened and pick up our friendship from where he'd left off. I tried to talk to him about it once, but he dismissed my expressions of concern with a dramatic shake of his head and an adamant, 'Don't even go there, Binnie, my friend. Don't even go there.'

And all the time our friendship deepened. I've never liked that word *soulmate* with its sentimental, other-worldly connotations. I'd give up writing before I'd allow it on to the pages of one of my novels. But that's what he was. I know what normal healthy companionship is. I know what normal healthy sexual attraction is. I know what normal healthy family relationships are. And this was like none of these. There's another word that is so loaded with overtones and resonances that I'm reluctant to use it. But I'll overcome that reluctance and say it. I *loved* Byron Abercrombie-Brydges. I've had many acquaintances since those days: people I've liked a great deal and who've liked me. There have been several women in my life whose company I have enjoyed: good women that I wish I had treated better than I did. And I'm married to a woman I love: a good woman to whom I've been faithful. But my friendship with Byron was different from all of these. It was a unique, once-in-a-lifetime, never-to-be-forgotten bond between two young men with an insatiable appetite for life and a passion to master the craft of writing.

After the spring break, I returned to Oxford at the end of April looking forward to resuming our friendship and assuming that our star would remain in the ascendancy as we continued our shared quest for literary fame. But as soon as I saw Byron on the first day of the Trinity term, I knew that he had changed. Something was different. The glow that had seemed to light up his pale skin had faded, leaving only a deathly pallor. His extravagant attire, the flamboyant clothes that matched and highlighted his unique personality, now hung on his body, looking nothing more than a bizarre assortment of ill-matched and ill-fitting garments. But it was his eyes – those darting eyes that had encompassed and engaged an entire roomful of people in seconds – that shocked me most of all. They were dull, lifeless, half-closed, as if attempting to shut out the light of day rather than opening to observe the bright world around him.

He said he wanted to talk and suggested that we walk across the road to the same café where we'd eaten breakfast on the first morning. We didn't order any food, but I drank a cappuccino and he took tiny sips from a glass of water.

'Binnie, there's no easy way to tell you this.' He spoke in a whisper, not just because he didn't want to be overheard, but because he lacked the strength to speak any louder. 'I was diagnosed HIV positive a while ago, and now it's developed into full-blown AIDS. I knew about it before I came up to Oxford. I had a fair idea that I was unlikely to survive long enough to reach graduation. But I wanted at least to get a taste of university life. And I wouldn't have missed this for the world.'

I wanted to protest. I wanted to grab him by the shoulders, shake him and tell him not to be stupid. Tell him that there must be some mistake and that he'd get better with the right treatment. But my brain held my emotions in check, told me just to shut up and listen, told me that, of course, he was telling the truth. The truth that I should have sussed months ago if I'd had any sense. It was my anger at my own stupidity as much as the shock of what I was hearing that brought the tears to my eyes.

'Come on, Binnie. We don't want any of that nonsense. The doctor's told me I haven't got long. But it's not over yet. I think I can manage to stay up in Oxford for another couple of weeks. Let's not worry about lectures and tutorials. We can just concentrate on becoming writers...' He paused and something of the old light came back into his eyes, '... and maybe even doing a bit of partying.'

I drew the palms of my hands down my cheeks to dry my eyes, and muttered a string of profanities as I tried to cover my embarrassment and pull myself together.

'I know how you feel. And you're right. It's crap. But that's life. And you've been a real friend.' He put his hand on my shoulder and looked at me with a smile that threatened to break my heart and set me crying again. 'I didn't want to talk about it and you never raised the subject, but you must have known I'm gay. Having a straight guy like you as a friend has helped to keep me away from temptation. The last thing I wanted to do was to get involved with another guy and infect him with this rotten disease. You've been my guardian angel, or my conscience, or something like that.'

And the crazy thing was that I'd never given a thought to his sexuality. With hindsight, it was obvious from so many things about him. Maybe it was my naivety or the relatively sheltered upbringing I'd had. More likely, his larger-than-life personality, his passionate love of literature, his fierce determination to be a writer, his faithful friendship that was like no other I'd ever experienced – all of these loomed so large that they obscured everything else.

The days that followed are a blur in my mind. The only thing that I'm completely sure about is that he devoted neither time nor energy to pursuing his ambition to be a writer. Study gave way to an exhausting round of late-night parties that was punctuated by daylight hours when we were both almost too exhausted to sleep. But somehow, Byron managed to revive each evening as the light faded and the celebrations began all over again. No ageing rock star ever staged a farewell tour to greater acclaim than he received from the admiring audiences who filled bars and clubs to say goodbye in those first two weeks of the Trinity term in 1990. Students whose minds should have been focused on essays and exams took time off to say their goodbyes to someone whose like they doubted they would ever see again.

But inevitably his limited store of energy ran out. His father came to pick him up late on a Thursday evening to take him home. I walked with him to their car, supporting him with my arm around his waist and easing him into his seat. He looked at me through the window of the car as they drove off and mouthed the word 'thanks'. I was sure it would be the last time I would ever see him and I headed straight to the nearest pub, where I spent what was left of the night drinking myself into oblivion. I came round at five o'clock the following morning, lying on a park bench with a filthy headache and feeling utterly miserable. It was well into the afternoon before I wandered into college to attend a tutorial to which I'd been summoned by a tutor growing impatient with my frequent absences. The porter called my name as I passed his lodge and waved a piece of paper at me. It was a phone message from Byron's mother asking me to call her as soon as possible.

She answered immediately the phone rang.

'I hope you don't mind me calling you,' she said. 'But Byron's been telling us how helpful your friendship has been to him. We wondered if you'd be willing to come as soon as possible. He may not have long.'

I said that I'd come straight away and she gave me their address, adding that I shouldn't come by public transport but take a taxi which they'd pay for.

Two hours later I arrived at the exclusive Thames-side residence of the Abercrombie-Brydges family.

'There's something troubling him,' Byron's father said as he led me upstairs to Byron's bedroom. 'He says there are things he needs to talk to you about.'

He left us alone and I pulled a chair up by the bed. I was shocked at how quickly my friend had deteriorated in just twenty-four hours. He beckoned me to come closer so that I could hear him. His breathing was laboured and his words were barely more than a whisper. I will never know how lucid he was in those moments, whether that bedroom overlooking the Thames became a true confessional for someone who needed to unburden his soul, or whether what I was hearing was nothing more than the confused ramblings of a dying young man whose brain was no longer capable of rational thought. What I do know is that Byron Howard John Abercrombie-Brydges was racked with guilt – guilt for who and what he was, guilt for having been born into a world that was so broken that he could survive only by losing himself in a life of self-indulgent hedonism, guilt for his own wrongdoing, guilt for those he might have hurt. If I'd been a priest, I would have offered a prayer, anointed him with holy oil, granted him absolution for his sins, promised him a place in heaven. But I was – *I am* – just another human being, trying to make the best of things most of the time and hoping to find some way of muddling through when it all goes wrong. All I could do was hold his hand and listen until he drifted off to sleep.

I stayed with the Abercrombie-Brydges family over the weekend, spending most of that time by Byron's bedside, sometimes keeping a lone vigil, sometimes with one or both of his parents sitting beside me.

The picture of their son that emerged from our whispered conversations was not what I had anticipated. The family were devout Catholics and Byron, their only offspring, had been a quiet and shy child who was unusually earnest in his observance of the faith he had inherited. For a number of years, he'd even talked about entering the priesthood. All that had changed when, at the age of seventeen, he tried to tell his parents about his sexuality. It was a revelation that his father in particular found difficult to cope with. His harsh words and angry reaction to what his son had tried to share led to a bitter argument and a breach in their relationship that resulted in Byron leaving home.

For almost two years he made no contact with his family until he suddenly turned up unannounced, asked their forgiveness for the pain he'd put them through, and pledged to them that though the priesthood was no longer a vocation he could follow, he was determined to live a celibate life. His father and mother welcomed him home and they, in turn, apologised for their initial response. Their delight at his return and his subsequent acceptance to read English at the University of Oxford was tempered by the news that he'd been diagnosed as HIV positive. But they promised each other that whatever the future brought, they would face it together as a family. And that was exactly what they'd tried to do.

Byron died at nine minutes past seven on a Monday evening while a gentle breeze carried the sound of birdsong and the lapping of the softly flowing river through the open window. The priest who had administered the last rites was still by the bedside when Byron's breathing stopped. His mother and father knelt together holding hands and praying quietly. I stood a little behind them, grieving wordlessly for the loss of my best friend.

Later that evening as I was getting ready for bed, his mother knocked on the bedroom door and handed me an envelope that he'd instructed her to give to me only after he had died.

'He dictated it to me before you got here. He didn't have the strength to write it himself. So I know what it says, of course. But you'll want to be alone when you read it.'

As soon as I closed the door I sat on the edge of the bed and read the letter, mouthing the words quietly to myself.

Binnie,

I thought about addressing you as 'my dear old friend', even though we're both just young men and we've known each other for such a short time. And you have been the best friend I ever had. But Byron and Binnie had a great ring to it. So I'll settle for just calling you 'Binnie' as I've done ever since we met.

I've no doubt that my parents will have filled you in on a few things about me and about us as a family. That should have helped you to understand me a little better. Even if I hadn't succumbed to AIDS, I suspect that I would never have reached the 'three score years and ten' that most folk seem to regard as their right. I'm grateful for the time I've had, but I've found it difficult to live with the world and with myself. Everything seems so out of kilter. There's something wrong with it all and it troubles me that I've never managed to find an answer that's adequate. There's only so long anyone can run from the truth before things catch up with them. And it's certainly caught up with me. Maybe one day you'll find some kind of answer, but I know it's beyond me.

And maybe now you'll understand why I love Childe Harold's Pilgrimage so much. I know you found it hard going when we read it through together. (OK, I will admit that it is very long and just a bit boring in parts.) But I want you to do me a favour. My folks have agreed – with some persuasion – to put a verse from it on my tombstone and I'd really like you to read that verse at my funeral. It's the 126th verse of the fourth canto. Some folk might not like it. But I think you'll agree that it's a suitable epitaph for me.

Thanks for being my friend. You'll never know how
much you mean to me.
Byron

I put the letter back in the envelope and wiped a tear from my eye. The emotional and physical demands of the last few days suddenly hit me. I lay down and fell asleep until late the next morning.

A week later, at a service in a private chapel, with only the priest who officiated, Byron's parents and a few members of their extended family present, I recited the verse that he'd requested and that I'd committed to memory.

> Our life is a false nature – 'tis not in
> The harmony of things, – this hard decree,
> This uneradicable taint of sin,
> This boundless upas, this all-blasting tree,
> Whose root is earth, whose leaves and branches be
> The skies which rain their plagues on men like dew –
> Disease, death, bondage, all the woes we see –
> And worse, the woes we see not – which throb through
> The immedicable soul, with heart-aches ever new.

It was certainly not the kind of consoling stanza that I've heard read at funerals so often since that day. It pointed towards no heavenly landscape where angels with harps float past weightlessly on ethereal clouds. It gave no glimpse of pearly gates where the souls of the dead wait humbly and ask to be admitted. It tendered no comforting version of reality in which death means nothing and the dear departed have just gone into another room. It offered neither hope nor help, but simply presented a view of life as it is right here and now. It faced the hard reality that the poet Byron had described so beautifully and my friend Byron had experienced so painfully.

I returned to Oxford and spent the last few weeks of term trying to find my way back into university life. But I have spent the rest of my life hoping against hope that there might be a greater truth that answers and overcomes the bleak reality of the lines of poetry I had memorised and delivered at Byron's funeral, the lines that I have never been able to get out of my mind.

chapter 9
in the house of friends
1990

It was a warm and sunny autumn morning in September 1990 and I should have been looking forward to returning to university in ten days for the second year of my English Literature degree. In fact, I was lying on my bed at home in north London, with the curtains still drawn, trying unsuccessfully to get back to some kind of normality after the death of my friend and wondering whether I had the energy or even the desire to pick up my studies again. Oxford without the company of Byron Abercrombie-Brydges was an unappealing prospect.

The telephone was ringing annoyingly in the hallway downstairs and I was about to bury my head in the pillow in an attempt to shut out the noise when it stopped. Someone had answered it and I could go back to staring at the ceiling. To my dismay, I heard my mother's voice saying, 'Hold on. I'll get him for you.' That was the last thing I wanted to hear. When she tapped on the bedroom door and called my name, I pretended to be asleep. But she wouldn't be put off.

'Alexander,' she insisted. 'It's for you. You need to come to the phone. It's Mr Potter. He's already left three or four messages for you and you haven't had the decency to reply. You need to speak to him now and he's only got a few minutes before his next class.'

I got up grumpily, made my way downstairs, and picked up the phone.

'Ah, you're a hard man to get hold of, Mr Alexander Binnie,' he said, good-naturedly, before his voice took on a more serious tone. 'I've heard a bit about what's happened and I can understand just how you must be feeling. But it might help you to talk to someone. Now, just for old time's sake, why don't you come round to our house for a meal? We'll cook something special. And Amy will be delighted to see you. She often asks about you. You made a real hit with my daughter, you know.'

There was something comforting about the sound of his voice and his genuine concern for me. In all the excitement of those early months at university, and then in my grief at Byron's death, I'd failed to keep in touch as I'd promised him. My discourtesy in neglecting to make contact hadn't lessened his interest in me. As low as I was at that moment, it was impossible not to feel a little better for his kindness. I accepted his invitation to dinner, much to the relief of my parents, who'd been worried about my state of mind and fearful that I might drop out of university.

Dinner with the Potter family that Saturday evening gave me the impetus I needed to begin to climb slowly out of the black hole into which I'd fallen. Mrs Potter, as she never failed to do, served up generous helpings of appetising home-cooked food. Amy, as the custom of the household dictated, was carefully helped into her special chair and given time to say her simple prayer of blessing before we were allowed to eat. Mr Potter, as the patriarch of the family, presided over the meal, making sure that each of us was included in the conversation. When our plates were cleared, he and his wife took their daughter to her room to settle her for the night before he and I sat down together in his study to talk.

'Now, there's no pressure,' he assured me. 'Take your time. Say as much or as little as you want. I'll listen and try not to give you too much advice.'

I started to say sorry for not taking time to write him a letter or give him a phone call from university, but he waved my apology aside. He was sure, he said with a knowing smile, that Oxford was far too much fun for young fellows like me to be thinking about their old teachers they'd just escaped from. 'But I'm guessing it wasn't much fun in those last few weeks,' he added. 'From what I've gathered, you've lost a very special friend.'

I nodded in agreement and sat quietly, not sure where to begin. But gradually, with some long pauses in which I struggled to contain my emotions, I tumbled out the story: my first meeting with Byron, our shared love of literature and our mutual aspiration to be writers, the attractions of the party scene, my shock at the change in his appearance at the beginning of the Trinity term, his revelation of the nature of his illness, the request from his parents for me to be present during his last days, the bleak verse from *Childe Harold's Pilgrimage* that I'd read at the funeral, and my apathy and sense of lostness since I'd returned home.

'I'm not really sure who I am or what I want do with my life any longer. You know I've always wanted to be a writer, but I wonder if there's any point in it now. Even if I managed to write a decent novel, all I would be doing is giving people a brief escape from the reality of life.'

Mr Potter pursed his lips and looked at me with a quizzical expression for a moment.

'Hmph... I wonder, I wonder. A brief escape? D'you think that's really the case?'

He didn't wait for an answer from me, but walked across the room and lifted a sheet of paper from his desk.

'Read this,' he said, handing it to me. 'I wrote it down just the other day. Something Edvard Munch – you know, he's the Norwegian artist who painted *The Scream* – once said. Apparently, he was a photographer as well as a painter. But clearly, he believed that painting could do something that photographs never could. Read it aloud, if you don't mind.'

He listened as I read the words that he'd written out in bold block capitals. He asked me to read them again, more slowly the second time.

THE CAMERA WILL NEVER COMPETE WITH THE BRUSH AND PALETTE UNTIL SUCH TIME AS PHOTOGRAPHY CAN BE TAKEN TO HEAVEN OR HELL.

He took the paper from me, slipped it carefully into an envelope, and then gave it back to me again.

'You keep it. And read it from time to time. Consider it your homework from your old schoolteacher. I guess photographers might disagree. But I think I know what Munch is trying to say. The camera can give us a sharply focused image of the world around us. Help us to see

114

reality from a particular angle. But it takes the painter's skill and imagination to help us see the truth of things. Take us to places we could never otherwise go; show us levels of reality we could never otherwise reach. *And that's the task of a writer, too.* A good novel doesn't simply present us with everyday reality. It's the job of the newspapers to do that. But nor is it offering us an *escape* from everyday reality. That's the job of the light entertainment industry. It's well-told stories that take us to heaven or hell. It's stories that can become beacons penetrating the darkness. It's stories that can become windows letting the light in.'

He might have carried on further in this vein had Mrs Potter not brought in the coffee at that point with a plate filled with her home-made cakes and biscuits.

'Perfect timing, as always,' he told her. 'You've rescued Binnie from what was in danger of turning into a boring lecture that might have gone on all night.'

I protested that he was never boring when he talked about writing, but Mrs Potter said she knew her husband only too well and she was glad to have saved me from that fate. There were no further pertinent quotations or profound reflections on the nature of literature or anything else. The rest of the evening was taken up with something arguably even more important than either of those things – the simple human kindness of two older people with challenges enough of their own, and who expected nothing in return, to a young man who'd found himself almost overwhelmed by the loss of his first true friend.

As I was leaving, they asked how my parents were and I told them of the reconciliation that had taken place a year before when I'd met my grandparents for the first time. That led to a conversation about the unique nature of the relationship between grandparents and their grandchildren, something that they acknowledged wistfully they would never have the opportunity to enjoy.

'Be nice to them, Alexander,' Mrs Potter urged me as she hugged me when I said goodbye and thanked them for their hospitality. 'You're lucky to have them and they're lucky to have you. Make sure you pay them a visit now and then. And don't forget to pay us another visit next time you're home from Oxford.'

It was a passing but revealing comment from a woman who, without ever realising it, had been a surrogate grandmother to more than a few youngsters she and her husband had taken under their wing over the years. But I couldn't get her words out of my mind as I walked home that night. My grandparents were in their mid-eighties. They wouldn't be around for ever. And if I wanted to get to know them, I should do something about it now. By the time I got up next morning, I'd made up my mind. I was going to go to Bellmill and visit them.

My parents were surprised and delighted by my sudden surge of energy and unexpected decisiveness. So delighted, in fact, that my father made the phone call to them asking if they'd mind putting me up for a few days, paid the train fare, and even gave me some money to spend on my four-day trip to Scotland.

My grandfather met me on the Friday afternoon at Glasgow Central station where we caught a local train for the forty-minute journey to Bellmill before embarking on a mile's walk to the council estate where they'd lived since the 1960s. He'd never learned to drive, he explained as we walked at a brisk pace that might have taxed a man half his age. Owning a car just wasn't an option when they'd been younger. And by the time they could have afforded to buy something suitable for their needs, they'd got used to travelling by public transport. Besides, he added, walking was as good a way of keeping fit and healthy as anything he could think of. Occasionally, he admitted, he did get a little breathless. But that was just the effects of the coal dust that had penetrated his lungs after fifty years working underground. It didn't prevent him getting around and it had never stopped him blowing his cornet. He could still join in and march when they needed him, he said proudly, though at his wife's insistence he'd really retired from playing in the band.

The door was flung open as we walked up the path and my grandmother, who'd obviously been looking out for us, came hurrying down the steps to greet us.

'Alexander Binnie!' she exclaimed, throwing her arms around my neck. 'Our grandson! In our home! I never thought I'd live to see this day.'

Immediately we stepped into the house I could tell, not just from her flushed face and the marks on her apron where she wiped her hands quickly, but from the aroma coming from the kitchen, that she'd been busy getting a meal ready for my arrival. Fortunately, my father had forewarned me of the generous nature of working-class Scottish hospitality and advised me not to eat anything on the journey that might spoil my appetite for what would be set before me when we sat down to eat. We worked our way steadily through three ample courses and rounded off the meal with tea served in delicate china cups, and two large helpings of my grandmother's chocolate cake, a delicacy that my grandfather proudly declared to be 'the finest home-baked sponge cake in all of Scotland'.

Alec and Irene Binnie didn't expect me to sing for my supper, but they certainly did insist on hearing every detail of their only grandson's life story before we retired for the night. It was well past midnight when they gave the first indication that it might be time for bed. The flickering light from dying embers in the coal fire had almost disappeared when my grandfather eased himself up from his chair and drew our conversation to a conclusion.

'We'd better let this young man get some sleep, Irene. He must be tired after his journey and answering all our questions.' He turned and looked at me, his eyes glowing with pride. 'Old Sandy Binnie would be so pleased that someone in this family has got to Oxford university. It was such a disappointment to him when Bobby and me went down the pit. He always wanted his family to get on in life. It's taken a couple of generations, but I'm pretty certain he's looking down on us and smiling.'

'Well, maybe you'll tell me a bit more about him tomorrow,' I responded. 'We don't know anything about my mum's family. And until we met last year, I knew nothing about dad's family either. So there's a lot for me to learn.'

'You don't know what you're letting yourself in for,' my grandmother said as she showed me to my bedroom and gave me a hug. 'I would think you've discovered already on the journey from Glasgow that he loves to talk. Still, if you want to be a writer, he might just provide you with some interesting tales you can make use of in the future.'

The next day proved that she had not overstated her husband's ability to wax eloquent on the history of the Binnie family or his talent for telling a captivating tale. After breakfast, he and I set out on a walking tour of Bellmill. As we strolled through the town, he reeled off story after story of what had occurred wherever we happened to be standing at that moment. We stopped outside the supermarket that had replaced the grocer's shop where his father, Sandy, the first Alexander Binnie, had worked. We paused for a while in front of the spot where the *single end* had once stood, the tiny one-roomed home in which he and Bobby had been born and raised and from which their father had left to answer the call of king and country in 1914. Together we walked the length of the Main Street where, during the General Strike in 1926, he and his brother had marched past each other heading in opposite directions. He pointed wistfully at the words still visibly etched into the stone arch above the door of what had been the original Salvation Army hall, the place where he had found a faith that had sustained him through a lifetime. It was now an amusement arcade.

On the way home, he even added a new word to my vocabulary when he pointed out the *bing* on the edge of the town – the man-made hill formed from the waste material that had been thrown up from the now defunct Black Moss Colliery where he'd worked – and explained to me that the word *bing*, far from being just a bit of local slang, was actually an Old Norse word that had long ago fallen out of use in English but still survived in the Lowland Scots dialect. When I expressed my surprise at his knowledge of extinct languages, he laughed, gave a look of mock modesty, and admitted that he'd gone to the

119

library to look it up a few days earlier 'just to impress the Oxford undergraduate in the family'.

It was a confession all the more significant for the self-deprecating manner in which it was shared, and one that prompted me to reflect on my relationship to this man who was more than sixty years my senior and who'd lived a life that was so far removed from mine in almost every way. Perhaps I had more in common with him than I could ever have imagined. His opportunity for formal learning had been limited to a basic education that had ended when he was fourteen. But he was far from illiterate, and he was certainly not dim-witted. What would he have made of himself if he'd had the opportunities I'd had in life? And now, in his ninth decade, he still had the kind of curiosity that would drive him to the local library to check the derivation of an obscure dialect word that he knew I'd never have heard before.

Then there was, as my grandmother had pointed out and I had observed for myself, his almost compulsive desire to hold a listener's attention with a convincing tale. My father was largely taciturn, more of a doer than a communicator, who would often lose himself in his own thoughts. And neither of my parents had any talent for storytelling. Had I inherited my own impulse to be a writer – a storyteller – from my grandfather? Humility, people have often told me, has never been my strong suit. But in that moment I felt humbled, seeing more clearly than ever before that the gifts I possessed were just that – *gifts* – talents that I'd been given, that I'd inherited from others. And whatever initial academic success I'd achieved by gaining a place at a prestigious university was largely owing to the good fortune of the time and place and circumstances into which I'd been born. More than that, I felt *connected* – joined by ties of family and genetics to generations who'd gone before me. If our family had emigrated to America at the beginning of the twentieth century, rather than remaining on this side of the Atlantic, I would probably be proudly identifying myself as Alexander Binnie IV.

There were still more surprises to emerge that day. Back home in the evening, after we'd finished our meal, my grandfather announced that there was something he wanted me to have. He went over to the sideboard and brought out three A4 exercise books with blue covers.

'I'd like you to have these,' he said, handing them to me one by one. 'You might find them interesting. In this one I've put everything I know about my father – your great-grandfather Sandy. In this one there's our story – your grandmother and me. And this last one's about your dad, though sadly there's a big gap in it. You know… all those years we weren't in touch with each other. I've tucked some old photos in each of them. I'm no writer, but maybe you'll be able to make something of them one day.'

'You're just trying to sound modest,' my grandmother teased him. 'Tell the boy the truth. You're very proud of what you've written in those old school jotters.'

'Well, if I am,' he laughed, 'we need to deal with my pride. It's the worst of sins. And that reminds me, there's something I need to say to you, Alexander. Irene and I never miss the Sunday morning service. It's what we call our Holiness Meeting. It's a weekly discipline for us. We'd be very happy if you chose to come with us, but there's no pressure on you to do that. You're our guest and you must feel free to stay at home, or go for a walk, or do whatever you want to do.'

I'd never so much as heard of a 'holiness meeting', let alone been to one in my life. Nor had I the remotest idea what happened at one, though I suspected it would be either embarrassing or spooky and I was sure it wasn't the kind of activity that I'd want to be involved in on a Sunday morning. Since they'd given me the option, it wouldn't be difficult to politely decline the invitation without giving any offence. Somehow, that thought didn't transmit from my brain to my mouth and, to my surprise, I heard myself saying, 'Sure, I'll come with you.'

As I lay in bed that night, flicking through the pages of the exercise books and glancing at the photos he'd given me, my thoughts were darting backwards and forwards. There was a sense of belonging I'd never felt before as I began to appreciate that I wasn't just the only child of Ecky and Sue. I was part of a family about which I had so much to learn, a family that reached back into the past, a family whose members had played their small part in the history of the nation. But there was a sense of unease about what was awaiting me in the morning. What had I let myself in for by agreeing to accompany my hosts to a religious gathering, the purpose of which, I guessed from my grandfather's words, was to expose the truth about our thoughts and motives?

All these years later, I'm still not sure what to make of that Sunday morning. My grandparents were delighted that I'd accepted their invitation and they insisted on introducing me proudly to their friends in the congregation as their grandson 'who's about to start his second year at Oxford university'. So I'd been right about it being embarrassing. I'd been wrong, however, about it being spooky. With only one or two exceptions, the people around me seemed normal and there was nothing forced or hyper-spiritual about what was happening. The songs had tunes that were easier to sing than most of the hymns I'd endured in school assemblies. And, being seated next to my grandmother, who gave me a whispered running commentary as the service went along, I'd no trouble knowing when to stand up or sit down again.

Nonetheless, there were puzzling moments, particularly when it got to the sermon. The ninety or so people in the hall maintained a respectful silence throughout the twenty minutes given over to this homily, though I wasn't at all sure that this was the highlight of the morning for most of them. The Major speaking from the rostrum – my grandmother informed me of his title with a reverence that left me in no doubt of her respect for his rank – had a pleasant manner, but whatever holiness was, it was lost to me in a fog of religious jargon. His efforts to express it in words that would take hold of his hearers' imagination and enable them to apply it to their lives on a Monday morning seemed doomed to failure until his concluding, confident declaration.

'The wonderful truth is,' he said with conviction, lifting his head from his notes and looking across the congregation, 'we can not only be forgiven for our sinful thoughts and actions. We can also receive the power to overcome them.'

I was not among the handful of people who responded to his invitation to step forward and kneel at the front of the hall, presumably to receive the power of which he was speaking. Nor have I ever attended another Salvation

Army meeting in my life. In fact, I've been to relatively few church services of any kind since that day, other than weddings, christenings and funerals. But that confident assertion has lodged itself in my mind. Receive a power to overcome our sinful thoughts and actions? If only… if only that were possible.

Years later, at a forum that brought together painters, musicians and writers with the intention of stimulating creativity by exchanging ideas from our different disciplines, I shared, somewhat disparagingly as I recall, the memory of that moment with three other people in a buzz group. The painter on my left found it amusing and speculated that the incredulous expression that must have shown on my face when I first heard those words would have given him the opportunity for an interesting portrait. The man sitting opposite me – a jazz musician – listened thoughtfully and then related the story of a little-known and seemingly unremarkable incident in the life of one of his great heroes.

Back in the 1940s, Charlie Parker, the legendary tenor saxophone player, was returning to New York's Grand Central Station with a group of his fellow-musicians early on a bitterly cold winter morning after playing a late-night gig at a venue on the outskirts of the city. As they emerged from the station, they came upon a Salvation Army Band playing a little untunefully on the street corner. Having been up all night, they were all anxious to get back to their hotel and head straight to bed. But Parker, to their surprise and annoyance, insisted on stopping to listen. His companions hurried on and left him standing on his own. Months later one of the group who'd been with him that morning went to hear him play in a club on Fifty-Second

Street. Charlie Parker noticed him in the audience, gave him a wink and, in the middle of his solo, incorporated a snatch of one of the tunes they'd heard The Salvation Army Band playing.

'I've always loved that story,' my jazz musician friend concluded. 'It says something about Charlie Parker and his willingness to listen and learn from what everyone else considered an unlikely quarter. It reminds me that it's never wise to make rigid boundaries in art or in life. You never know where you're likely to catch a glimpse of truth, or hear a rumour of beauty.'

But on that Sunday morning, sitting beside my grandparents, I was still too young, and the pain I felt at the loss of my friend was still too raw, for me to reflect with such maturity and humility on the extravagant offer that had been made by the preacher. All I could think was that if there had been such a power at the heart of the universe, the world would be a less dangerous place and Byron Abercrombie-Brydges would still be living in the room opposite me when I got back to university in a few days' time. Besides, I was only beginning to process everything I'd heard from my grandfather the previous day. The naïve idealism of Sandy Binnie when he'd left his family to enlist in a conflict whose causes he did not understand and whose consequences he could never have imagined; the horror of life in the trenches on the front line in France; the physical and mental hurt my great-grandfather had brought back from his time in the British Army; the different paths taken by his sons as they'd sought to find an answer for the pain and injustice that had so damaged and ultimately destroyed their father; the decades-long rift between my own father and his father over something as innocent as participation in a game of football; the cruel injury that had ended a young man's dreams of sporting glory. I had too many questions to be satisfied with a one-sentence answer in a twenty-minute sermon.

Even now, thirty years later, I have more questions than answers, more gaps in my understanding of life than neat and tidy theories with which to fill the holes. But what I have never lost since that weekend spent in Bellmill before I began my second year at Oxford is the sense of being linked to those generations that went before me and the awareness that I too will one day become just another member of those generations who are part of history. And I was soon to learn that the transition from present to past can happen swiftly and with little warning.

I never saw my grandparents again after I waved them goodbye at Glasgow Central Station on that final Monday morning. Three months after my visit, my grandfather had a heart attack while marching with his beloved Salvation Army Band and never recovered consciousness. If he'd been allowed to choose the circumstances of what he would have called his 'promotion to glory', he could not have chosen a more suitable passing. My grandmother died two months later. I'm convinced that after more than sixty years of marriage to the only man she'd ever given herself to, she saw no point in delaying her reunion with her husband in an eternity of which she was utterly confident. I think of them often and wonder what they would make of what I have become and who I am.

chapter 10
life and death as an undertaker
1992–94

I graduated from university in the summer of 1992, having plodded through the second and third years of my studies with little enthusiasm and just enough application to avoid embarrassing my parents by dropping out altogether. I emerged from the halls of academia with an unspectacular and largely undeserved lower second-class honours degree, usually shortened in university parlance to 'a 2.2', and consequently often referred to by students, employing rhyming slang in a collective and affectionate nod to the popular former Archbishop of Cape Town, as a 'Desmond'. It is an incontrovertible fact – as I quickly discovered – that apart from the teaching profession, for which I knew I was singularly unsuited, employers at the end of the 1990s were neither waiting for nor welcoming to an English Literature graduate in possession of a 'Desmond'. Particularly one who naïvely revealed in interviews that his main ambition was to be a novelist.

I did manage to secure a temporary position as a copywriter for an advertising agency with the promise that it could lead to a permanent post if my work was up to scratch. It came to an end after three months by mutual agreement, with my boss telling me that I didn't have the aptitude for what they were looking for, while I insisted that what they were looking for was someone without scruples and willing to be a bare-faced liar rather than a decent human being with the talent and values of a writer.

After almost a year of unsuccessful and soul-destroying job-hunting, help came from an unexpected quarter.

'Look son, here's a suggestion,' my father said one Saturday morning, as he finished his coffee and put down his newspaper, having watched me filling in yet another job application at the kitchen table. 'Why don't you come and work for me for six months? We're short-handed with a couple of staff on long-term sick. You could do four days a week. That'd leave you a couple of days to do the writing thing. It'll help me out. And it'll give you a bit of money and some breathing space to work out what you want to do in the long run. If you really don't like it and you find you can't work with me, you can quit. At least you'll be a little less broke than you are at the moment and I'll be no worse off than I am now.'

The thought of working in what was now the family business had never occurred to me and the prospect of doing so filled me with more than a few misgivings. But beggars can't be choosers and a young man with not a penny to his name can't turn down the chance of gainful employment, even if it means working with his father. I accepted his offer, albeit with some reservations.

To the surprise of both of us, it was a working relationship that functioned with barely a hitch. I had no desire to get involved in the complexities of running the company and no ambitions to take over the business from him, so there was no reason for any rivalry between us. I was content to do whatever was asked of me.

At first, the discipline of having to be awake and dressed before seven o'clock every morning was irksome to someone who retained a student mindset about getting out of bed while it was still dark, and it took me a while to get used to wearing a suit and tie throughout the working day. After a few months, however, I got used to it, to the point where it became the new normal for me. To my surprise, I began to feel comfortable in an environment in which I'd never imagined myself working.

There were benefits for a would-be writer that as an overconfident but callow youth I'd never thought about. Every day I met men and women from all walks of life who had only one thing in common: they had lost someone who had been important to them. At moments like that, in the throes of grief, confronted with the sudden realisation that life is far less certain and predictable than we like to think, the masks behind which we hide are dropped and we can be glimpsed for who we truly are. Some of us manage to stand strong, resolute and stoical in the face of death. Others crumple helplessly before its ruthless finality. The years I spent working alongside my father gave me an insight into human nature with its strengths and weaknesses that few other occupations would have afforded me. It also tutored me in the endlessly fascinating intricacies of the ways in which people communicate with each other – those infinite combinations of words and pauses and gestures and looks and touches that make up what we glibly dismiss as 'small talk'. But those seemingly casual conversations are the very currency of relationships that each of us spends so extravagantly and receives back from others with interest. And those are the transactions that are so infuriatingly difficult to capture with any degree of authenticity in the printed word.

In short, I learned, as all of us must do – but writers, perhaps, to an even greater degree – to live life on two levels simultaneously. To be always fully present in the moment as we interact with the person in front of us, and yet mentally and emotionally to be taking a step back and observing what is happening so that in a quieter space we can remember and reflect on all that has taken place. In short, I learned to look and listen as never before, and then to squirrel away everything that I'd picked up. Gradually I filled several notebooks with revealing snippets of conversation, curious reactions to events and uncharacteristic behaviours by people whose conduct would previously have appeared predictable and ordinary to their family and close friends. It would have seemed a random, even bizarre, assortment of scribblings to anyone who had flicked through the pages of those untidy *collectanea*. But it became grist to my writer's mill. And from that myriad of encounters with people facing the reality of death and loss there are two that stand out in my mind and have an important place in my story.

I'd been working at Pomphrey's Funeral Directors for less than six months, when my father called me into his office and asked me to take a seat. His manner seemed unusually formal.

'What's the problem?' I asked, wondering if I'd done something wrong. 'I think I've completed the jobs you gave me to do.'

'Oh, you haven't done anything wrong,' he responded reassuringly. 'It's nothing like that. But I'm afraid I've got some bad news for you. I've just had a call from Mrs Potter to let me know that her husband's been killed in a road accident. Knocked off his bike by a speeding motorist, as far as I can gather.'

I was taken aback. It wasn't the first time I'd had to deal with the loss of someone who meant a lot to me. The death of Byron Abercrombie-Brydges had been painful. And the passing of my grandparents within months of each other and so shortly after I'd visited them had impacted me deeply. But Byron's illness had given me some warning of what was about to happen. And my grandparents were both well into their eighties. But Mr Potter had seemed to me to be somehow indestructible. Since I'd started working for my father and got into a proper routine, I'd been visiting the Potter family about every six weeks. They'd become a fixture in my life. Before I could reply, my father spoke again.

'Here's the thing. I think you should head round to see her now. She didn't exactly say so, but I'm pretty sure she'd like you to handle the funeral arrangements. Apart from the shock of losing her husband, she's got Amy to look after on her own now. She needs a bit of extra help beyond what we're normally able to give to folk. And I'd appreciate it if you'd take the lead on this one. You know them well and he's meant a lot to you over the years.'

It was the first funeral for which I took responsibility and it's an experience I'll never forget. I thought that I'd known the Potters long enough to have a fair estimation of the kids like me they must have helped over the years. It turned out that I'd no real idea of just how many lives

131

they'd touched. When the hearse drove through the gates of the cemetery on that wet and windy late autumn morning, I couldn't believe the number of people who were lining the avenue that led up to the crematorium, oblivious to the driving rain. Even my father, who'd attended literally hundreds of funerals, was moved when they spontaneously burst into applause as we drove slowly past.

Those who couldn't find room inside stood three and four deep outside the chapel as the service proceeded and the rain continued to pour down. And the professional detachment I'd been trying to perfect completely deserted me when I remembered the cruel attempts at humour by an immature fifteen-year-old schoolboy who had completely failed to recognise the true stature of the bald man who taught him history and rode a squeaky bicycle to and from school every day. It was the only occasion in all the time I worked for Pomphrey's Funeral Directors that I cried at a funeral.

After the service I took Mrs Potter and Amy back to their home, intending to leave them on their own after I'd seen them safely indoors. Mrs Potter, however, asked me to come in for a few minutes. There were some things she wanted to speak to me about, and something she'd like me to have. When I'd helped her to take Amy to her room, she told me of her plans over a cup of tea.

'Amy and I will sell the house and move to the south coast. My sister lives in that part of the country. She's a retired teacher. She's on her own and she's always said that if anything were to happen to Bill, we should move in with her. She's good with Amy and she'd be happy to help me to look after her.'

When we'd finished our tea, she took me into the small back bedroom that her husband had used as his study. It was lined with bookshelves, every one filled with volumes that he'd collected and read over a lifetime.

'I'd really be grateful if you'd help yourself to any of his books. And I'd like you to have this.' She pointed to a large cardboard box sitting on the desk. 'It's all his papers, all the stuff he's been writing over the years. It'd be too much for me to go through it. And he mentioned several times that he'd like to give it to you when he passed on. You know he thought the world of you. He told me once that you were the son he'd never had and the writer he wished he could have been.'

For the second time that day I failed to keep my emotions in check. I dried my eyes and hugged her and told her that I'd be honoured to accept such a gift.

'And, if I ever make it as a writer,' I added, 'I'll owe it all to your husband.'

My gratitude was genuine and my words were sincere, though I little realised how true they would turn out to be.

The second incident that stands out in my memory from those days as an undertaker opened the door to an unexpected but revealing encounter with my family's past. It was November 1994 and I'd been working in the family business for a little over a year. One morning my first appointment was with a woman in her mid-sixties, a Mrs Kirstie Levens, who'd come into the office to arrange the funeral of her mother, Mrs Morag McDonald. My father had emphasised to me in my first few months the importance of listening carefully to people's names, recording them accurately and, whenever it was appropriate, to make a polite comment. 'Do anything you

133

can to get the name firmly into your head,' he'd tell me over and over again. 'After all,' he'd explain, 'it's never a good thing for an undertaker to get the name wrong and risk burying the wrong person!' Anxious to follow his wise counsel, I remarked to Mrs Levens that both she and her mother were blessed with good Scottish names, adding that my own family hailed from north of the border.

'My folks came down from Scotland in the thirties to find work,' she responded. 'Dad's just had his ninety-seventh birthday last month and he's not so mobile these days. I don't think he'll be strong enough to attend the funeral. In fact, I'm not sure how long he'll keep going now that Mum's gone. They've been together for over sixty years. His short-term memory is going, but he's still got vivid memories of life in Scotland – he still calls it home even after all these years – and especially of his time in the army. If I'd a pound for every time he's told the story about the time he ran out of church as soon as the minister said "Amen" to go and join the army, I'd be a rich woman. And his accent seems to get broader the older he gets and the more he tends to live in the past.'

She paused to take her handkerchief out of her handbag and wipe a tear from her eye. I'd had enough experience of moments like this to recognise that I needed to give her time to talk before we pressed on with the practicalities of the funeral.

'He made us laugh the other night. He was talking about the things he'd seen in France early in the First World War and insisted that he'd seen "a statue o' a wumman an' a wean danglin' fae the top o' a church".' She shook her head and smiled as she tried to do justice to his

134

Scottish brogue. 'My husband jokingly suggested that they'd probably given the troops an extra tot of rum that day to get them ready to fight. But he was having none of it. Started to get a little annoyed at not being believed…'

She stopped herself and apologised for 'going on so much'. I assured her that I understood her need to talk and gave her a moment to compose herself before we finalised the remaining details. As she was leaving, she asked me to pass on her regards to my father and enquired how long I'd been working in the family business. I explained that my employment was intended to be temporary and that I hoped to make a career out of writing.

'Well, my parents didn't have a great education themselves,' she said. 'But they were both voracious readers. They always made sure that their children were encouraged to read. It's a habit that we carried into adult life. So I'll be looking out for your novel when it's published.'

I suggested that she shouldn't hold her breath as we shook hands and she left my office. I had another bereaved family waiting to see me almost immediately and gave no more thought to our conversation until late that evening when I was reflecting on the day and adding my customary jottings to my *collectanea*. I smiled to myself as I wrote down the words, 'a wumman an' a wean danglin' fae the top o' a church'. As I did so, it brought to mind something I vaguely remembered reading in one of the exercise books my grandparents had bequeathed to me when I'd visited them four years earlier. I'd glanced quickly at them on the train on the journey back to London and put them in a drawer when I got home, fully intending to read through them properly when I had time. I'd never got round to it.

I went to the drawer where I'd put them and picked out the one relating the life of my great-grandfather. I turned over the pages and scanned the neat copperplate handwriting until I found the passage I was looking for. I *had* remembered it correctly. There, halfway down the page, was the paragraph relating Private Sandy Binnie's arrival at a military camp in the village of Bouzincourt and describing the strange sight of the statue of the Madonna and Child, glinting in the morning sun, and still clinging precariously to the top of the basilica in Albert, despite the efforts of the German artillery. *That had to be what Mrs Levens' father had been talking about.* And if it was, could he have been in that camp at the same time? Was it possible that he'd met my great-grandfather?

My interest was piqued. I abandoned my plan to go to bed before midnight, made myself a cup of strong coffee to keep me awake, and settled down to read carefully through the part of the book that contained everything my grandfather Alec had been able to find out about his father's time as a soldier. It didn't take me long to find something that gave extra credence and even added a new possibility to the picture that was taking shape in my mind. For there, right on the first page of the chapter I was reading – a page I had skipped past the last time I'd held the flimsy but precious document in my hand – was the story of my great-grandfather heading straight from church with two younger Boys' Brigade leaders at the end of the Sunday morning service to catch a bus into Glasgow and enlist in the British Army. Was Kirstie Levens' father one of those two eager young men who had taken their lead from someone a few years older, someone they'd looked up to? There was certainly a gap in their ages, but it wasn't so big as to render my theory impossible. It was certainly worth checking out. Or was I just allowing my imagination to get the better of me? Was all this nothing more than one of those bizarre coincidences that life throws up from time to time?

I held my curiosity in check until the week after the funeral before calling Mrs Levens. I told her of the family history my grandfather had compiled and of my conjecture that her father and my great-grandfather might have met, might even have known each other. She was immediately interested.

'Well, there's nothing Dad loves more than talking about his days in the army. I don't think it would upset him if you asked him about it. Why don't you come round and chat to him? Just one thing you need to remember when you're talking to him. His proper name's Robert McDonald. But he insists on being called Rab. That's what he was always called back in Scotland. And despite my mum's constant nagging at him that he should settle for Rob after they came south, he was adamant that Rab was good enough for him.'

I responded that I'd be happy to respect her father's wishes regarding how he liked to be addressed, since I had to put up with my mother calling me Alexander even though I was much more comfortable with Alex, and we agreed that I'd call round the following afternoon.

Rab McDonald insisted on getting up with the help of his Zimmer frame and standing to greet me when I arrived. He knew only that I wanted to talk to him about his time as a soldier, and he'd gone to the trouble of wearing his regimental tie and putting on a jacket to which his First World War medals were pinned. He eased himself slowly back into his armchair and I was about to read the relevant passages in the exercise book I had with me, but as soon as I showed him some old sepia photographs that I'd brought with me and mentioned my great-grandfather's name his eyes lit up in recognition.

'Sandy Binnie! You're his great-grandson? Oh my...' His voice wavered for a moment and his daughter reached across and took hold of his hand. 'Aye, I knew Sandy Binnie, right enough. He was our BB captain. A good man. Must ha' been ten or eleven years older than ma pal Geordie and me. But we really looked up to him. He brought us young fellas on, gave us responsibility, encouraged us to be leaders. Even tried to get us tae talk like he did – proper posh English, you know. You can tell he didnae ha'e much success wi' that. When we knew he was goin' tae join the army, we were never goin' tae stay behind.'

His account of enlisting and of the early months of training that followed was filled with happy memories. His face became animated and the years seemed to drop away as he described a time of youthful innocence and painted vivid word pictures of training camps deep in the countryside that had offered an Eden-like environment for young men who'd lived all of their short lives up to that point in the industrial heart of Scotland. Long days of physical exercise in the open air and meals shared around communal tables gave little hint of what was to come. His expression altered when he recalled their departure from British shores and their time in France. Their life in Paradise was at an end. They had been cast out into a world where they would have reason to fear that malevolent forces were in control.

The one moment of light relief in his increasingly depressing tale came when he confirmed that he had indeed been in the camp at Bouzincourt with my great-grandfather.

'See,' he said, turning to his daughter, 'I wasn'ae wrang aboot the wumman an' the wean.'

Our amusement was abruptly ended as he went on to speak of conditions in the trenches and life on the front line. It was a long and sorry tale of young men maimed and killed before they'd had a chance to live, their guileless innocence swept away in the hideous tide of war. He'd been there that morning on the Somme at the beginning of July 1916 when the Second Battalion of the Highland Light Infantry went over the top and walked into the inferno of No Man's Land. He'd seen my great-grandfather, who'd been up ahead of him in the attack, being carried back to the trenches by the stretcher-bearers. It was, he said with a shake of his head and a barely stifled curse for which he quickly apologised, one of the worst moments of his life.

'There was nae rhyme or reason tae it. Why Sandy lost his leg, why ma pal Geordie who'd joined up wi' us was blown to bits, why I got out o' it unscathed – naebody knows why. It broke better men than me, an' it broke Sandy Binnie. Not just his body, but his very soul. When we got hame, it was impossible for anybody tae unnerstaun' whit we'd been through. We were only boys an' we wurnae ready for what we had tae face.'

He'd gone back to church at the end of the war, found comfort in his faith and resumed his involvement with the

Boys' Brigade. And he'd been part of a group from the church who'd tried unsuccessfully to persuade my great-grandfather to return to the flock and take up his place in the youth activities again. But he understood only too well why men like him came back different, why they'd found it impossible to believe again after all they'd seen and experienced.

'There was something terrible about it. Something so...' He struggled momentarily to find the word he was looking for. 'Something so... *evil*. And it got into you, twisted you out o' shape. It was hard not to let it destroy you. It ruined some of the men that came back. An' it had a big impact on their families. Families that just couldnae cope with the change in the man who'd come back. It took years for many o' them tae get o'er it. An' some never did.'

The old man shook his head ruefully and sighed. His daughter glanced at me with a look that said it was time to bring the conversation to an end. I carefully gathered up my photos and the exercise book I'd brought with me and thanked Rab McDonald for giving me his time. As I got to the door, he called me back. He'd one last thing that he wanted to say to me.

'Kirstie tells me you're a bit o' a writer.'

'For my sins,' I nodded, without giving any thought to my words. But he picked up on them.

'For your sins, eh?' he said, looking at me quizzically. 'For your sins? I'm thinkin' a' our stories are aboot oor sins. But try and make them better stories than the one I've just told you. And, for goodness' sake, gi'e them a happy endin'.'

I smiled and feigned agreement. I understood his desire for happy endings and there was no point in disagreeing with an old man who'd experienced all he'd been through in his life. The truth is, he was right about all our stories being about our sins. But that's the very thing that makes it so difficult to give them happy endings.

present

chapter 11
rough justice
2014

Tuesday 1st April, 2014. A day I won't forget. April Fools' Day. The annual opportunity for pranksters to amuse themselves by hoodwinking their unsuspecting victims. If only this was all a hoax. The door would suddenly swing open, someone would shout, 'April Fool', and I'd hear the sound of conspiratorial laughter from my friends who'd been in on the planning of such an elaborate practical joke and who'd be enjoying my embarrassment and confusion. But this is no joke, and the emotions I'm feeling cut far deeper than mere embarrassment. The door has just banged shut, the lock has been secured from the outside, and I'm lying on a rubber mattress in a shabby little room, twelve feet by eight feet, unfurnished apart from a couple of uncomfortable chairs, a tired-looking desk, a grubby sink, and a mirror covered in fingerprints and someone else's spit. Worse still, in the corner of the room there's an exposed loo that offers no privacy and that I'll be sharing with the man in the bunk above me, the man whose fingerprints and dried saliva are all over the mirror.

This, or another space exactly like it, will be my 'home' for up to twenty-three hours a day for the next eighteen months. The only consolation is that the relentless, migraine-inducing drumbeat of the last twelve hours has finally stopped. This is the inevitable conclusion of everything that's been happening since I got up at five o'clock this morning after a night of fitful sleep, nightmarish dreams and gut-churning anxiety about what the day would bring. My unsociable roommate clearly has no intention of communicating with me beyond his disapproving groan as I was ushered in and he realised that his hopes of a night undisturbed by the presence of another prisoner were gone. Even with the constant chorus of shouting and clattering from along the landing, I can still hear my heart beating loudly in my chest. I force myself to take long, slow breaths and try to reprise the events of the day in my mind. You never know, I think wryly, it could all be material for a novel. If I ever write again.

It's half past eleven when the judge pronounces his sentence. He's held it over from yesterday afternoon to give himself time to reflect on the gravity of my offence, consider any mitigating or aggravating circumstances, and decide on the severity of the punishment to be meted out to me. My hopes for leniency – perhaps a non-custodial or even suspended sentence – are quickly dashed when his opening remarks make it clear that he is far from impressed by either the character or the conduct of the prisoner standing before him in the dock.

In the event, he gives me three years, half to be served in custody and half out in the community under licence, providing I behave myself while I'm here. I manage to keep it all together until I catch a glimpse of my parents as the handcuffs are fitted around my wrists and I'm led out of the dock. It's a relief to head down the steps out of the courtroom and know that they won't be able to see me beginning to cry. The tears really begin to flow when two officers search me and confiscate my phone and my wallet in the tiny, bare cell where I wait to be transported to prison. It feels like everything is being taken from me, not just my possessions, but my self-respect and my very identity. No longer am I a literary celebrity, the man who's written a series of highly successful novels. I've just become a convicted criminal, a man who's been found guilty of a serious offence.

The indignities don't end there. I'm handcuffed to a guard, walked out to a waiting van and shoe-horned into one of several tiny claustrophobic cubicles that look and feel for all the world like the toilets on old-fashioned trains – except that there's no loo, just an uncomfortable seat. The others are already occupied by four prisoners, all old lags judging from the cynical banter passing between them and the way in which they seem to be taking all this in their stride. Only when I'm securely settled in are the handcuffs taken off and the doors of the van slammed shut. It's a long, slow journey and I get travel sick. I throw up over my trousers, but since I've barely eaten all day there's not as much vomit as there might have been. Small consolation, I know. But in a situation like this, you're grateful for any small mercy.

When we finally arrive here at the prison, I'm photographed and issued with an identity card that has my name, my picture, my date of birth and my prison number. The number is definitely all that really matters in this place. That's how I will be known from now on. The other details are nothing more than reminders of who I once was before I broke the law and justice took its course. After that, I'm searched again. This time it's a strip-search to make sure I don't have anything hidden inside my body. If only they knew how squeamish I am, how reluctant I've always been to allow even a properly qualified and sympathetic medical professional carry out a digital rectal examination, they could have saved themselves an unpleasant job and me an even more unpleasant experience.

Half an hour later I'm moved on again to another bare little room where I'm questioned to find out whether I have any suicidal tendencies and might need special surveillance to make sure I don't harm myself. I try to make a joke that anyone who'd just been searched as I was a few minutes before would consider a quick death the easier option, but my attempt at humour falls flat. They don't make jokes about that here, the unsmiling prison officer who's been interrogating me tells me curtly.

Then I take the longest and most unnerving walk of my life as I'm escorted to the induction wing. Every space we pass through is empty and hollow, every surface is hard and unyielding, everything about this place is bereft of anything that would offer even a faint reminder of normal human comfort. And every footstep resounds and echoes with a melancholy ring that's reminiscent of the tolling of a funeral bell. I'm handed into the care – though *care* is the last word I would associate with the life I anticipate here – of the officers in this wing who provide me with the essentials that every inmate is given on arrival: a couple of blankets, a pillow, a plastic mug and cutlery, three pairs of socks and underpants, three T-shirts and four jogging bottoms. I carry them in my arms into the cell, drop them on the floor, and throw myself on the bed.

There's nothing in my background, nothing in my family history, nothing in the past that I've told you about that would lead anyone to guess that I'd end up in this place at this time. But I've promised to tell you my story. The whole truth about me. And, whatever the past has been, *this is my present*. This is the culmination of what I've been doing and who I've been becoming for the last twenty years. And I know where this present begins. I can pinpoint the date and the time and the place when I left my past behind and took my first step on a road that has ultimately and inevitably brought me to this point.

chapter 12
writer's block
1997–2004

It's ten minutes past eight on the morning of Friday 2nd May 1997. I'm sitting in my office preparing to start work and listening to the news on the radio that Labour has emerged victorious in the General Election. Tony Blair will be heading to Buckingham Palace later in the day where the Queen will invite him to form Britain's next government. His visit, the party spokesperson confidently informs us, will signal a clear break with the past and usher in a new beginning for the country. I'm thinking to myself that old Alec Binnie, with his lifelong allegiance to the Labour movement, would have been pleased by this turn of events. And I'm steeling myself for the storm of fury that will blow in any minute with the arrival of my father, whose politics have moved significantly to the right of the generation who went before him. My thoughts are interrupted by the all too familiar ringing sound that punctuates my working days. I turn off the radio, pick up the phone and lapse straight into work mode.

'Good morning. Pomphrey's Funeral Directors. This is Mr Binnie junior speaking. How can I help you?'

'Well, Mr Binnie junior, I'm not dead, I'm glad to say. So I don't need the services of an undertaker. I would, however, like to speak to a writer.'

I immediately recognise the fruity tones of Harry Lipman, my literary agent for the past six months. Harry, I've come to realise, has a unique talent for conveying the news of yet another rejection from yet another publisher in such an upbeat manner that if you're not on your guard, the conversation can end with you being deluded into thinking that he's just shared some good news. The prospect of enduring my father's pessimism about the dark future of the nation is enough for one day. I'm certainly not ready for ten minutes of Harry's brand of unfounded but relentless and equally irritating optimism.

'Harry, just give me the bad news. I've got enough on my plate today putting up with my old man moaning about what he's convinced will be Labour's disastrous policies for small businesses like ours.'

There's a momentary pause and I get ready to receive the unwelcome truth.

'What bad news? There's no bad news from me, my boy.' Harry likes to remind his authors that they are his 'boys and girls' and certainly not his equals. 'I've got a publisher for your novel. They really like it. They think it's light years ahead of your previous stuff. They like it so much they want to put a bit of publicity behind it. They think it fills a niche in the market – readers in their late twenties and early thirties who are settling into a career, starting to raise families, realising that they've got something to learn from an older generation. They even like that crazy title of yours, *Bald Man on a Squeaky Bike*. So, it's all good.'

After all the disappointments I can hardly believe what he's telling me. I should be elated, but I just feel numb. Harry's waiting for a reply.

'Well, why don't you say something, Alex? You could try, "Thanks, Harry, for all the hard work you've been doing on my behalf." Something like that, maybe…'

'I'm sorry, Harry,' I stutter. 'Yeah, thanks. I do appreciate it. It's just hard to take it in after all the rejections.'

'Well, it's true. You're soon to be a published writer. And you should know by now that Harry Lipman never gives up. There's just one thing the publishers don't like. And I agree with them. Alexander Binnie sounds like someone who'd write a manual for people who're learning to play the bagpipes. It's too… well, too Scottish, to be honest. And it's old-fashioned. The kind of novel you've written needs an author whose name suggests, you know, a bit of style, a dash of confidence. A writer who's been around a bit, knows what life is all about. I've got one or two suggestions…'

For the next twenty minutes we toss ideas around, quickly dismissing the more ridiculous suggestions and slowly homing in on a few that sound like they might be genuine possibilities. We decide that Alex might be OK for what we need, but we come unstuck when we try to find the name to follow it. That's when Harry has what he calls one of his 'let's come at it from the other end' moments.

'Naah, Alex isn't right. Sounds too… too much like an MP or a local councillor. And you know what younger people think of them. Let's drop Alex and take the other half of your first name. Let's go for Zander. I think that's got the right ring to it. And it gives us a feel for what we want to follow it with.'

From there it takes us just a few minutes to come up with Bennings, which Harry says still keeps a link with Binnie and my roots. It allows him to engage in his penchant for self-congratulation.

'Zander Bennings.' He savours the words. 'Yes, we've got it. See, if you listen to Harry, you'll pretty well always be on the right track. You're a lucky boy that I had a space to take you on when you were looking for an agent who'd put you on the map.'

There's never any point in trying to get the upper hand when he's in this mood. And, since I'm forced to admit that I like the name as much as he does, we engage in some general chit-chat for a few minutes before Harry puts the phone down and gets on with whatever it is that literary agents do with their time. I, on the other hand, have a proper day's work ahead of me, for which I have suddenly lost my appetite. Undertaking as a profession quickly loses its attraction when you've just been told that you've got a book deal.

Somehow or other I manage to get through the next ten hours. I do my utmost to ignore my father's dire warnings about what the election result will mean for the business, try to focus on the tasks in hand, take particular care to sympathise with the bereaved customers, and make sure that I get the names of their deceased loved ones right. I'm relieved and exhausted when it gets to six o'clock. Few things are more draining than having to do a job that involves being nice to people and paying attention to detail when your mind is elsewhere.

When I eventually get home and have something to eat, I gradually begin to relax. I recall the voice on the radio that morning announcing that this is a day for breaking with the past and engaging with new beginnings. Breaking with the past, I recognise, will take some time for me. One novel accepted by a publisher, even with an upfront payment of £500, certainly won't provide me with enough money to live on. It would be foolhardy to immediately give up my reasonably well-paid job as an undertaker and vacate the lodgings provided free of charge in my parents' home. But I can embark on the new beginning that's presented itself. I can do that right now. I find the energy and enthusiasm to make a fresh start on some ideas I've had for a novel I've been working at off and on – though it's been more off than on in recent days – since the beginning of the year. There is hope. I'll be a writer yet. This might just be *my* time.

Twelve months later, despite my father's dire predictions, the business life of the nation hasn't ground to a halt and the newspapers are even commenting on the emergence of Cool Britannia under the leadership of its relatively youthful Prime Minister. On a personal level, the future isn't looking quite as bright for me as I'd hoped. *Bald Man on a Squeaky Bike* is selling reasonably well, but the figures are definitely nothing spectacular. The publisher's promise to back it with some attention-grabbing publicity has amounted to nothing more than a few low-key ads and a brief mention in their catalogue of new issues. I'm wondering if, in my excitement at getting my first novel published, I've fallen for a bit of flattery. Is what I'd imagined to be my first steps on an exciting new road nothing more than a short walk down a depressing cul-de-sac? Am I destined to spend the rest of my life as another forgotten author who manages to write a couple of mediocre novels in their spare time that hardly anybody will read?

Then, just as I'm settling for a future as an undertaker, things unexpectedly start to gather some fresh momentum. A journalist from one of the tabloids, at a loss for something to fill an inside page on a slow-news day, phones and asks to do an interview with me. The resulting article is a fairly run-of-the-mill piece, but it catches the attention of a more serious critic with one of the broadsheets who decides it's worth taking another look at the book, albeit somewhat belatedly. He likes it! *Bald Man on a Squeaky Bike* is one that's slipped under the radar, he says, and readers really should check it out. Sales begin to rise and, before I know what's happening, Harry Lipman's on the phone again to tell me that the publishers want a second book. It's just gone on from there.

That's really all there is to say about my career as a writer. Don't imagine for a minute that my reticence to say more on that subject is down to modesty. As I've often admitted, false modesty – or even the genuine article, for that matter – has never been a prominent characteristic of my personality. No, this story is meant to tell the truth about *me* – me as a man, as a human being – not to provide an insight into the craft of the novelist or to blow my own trumpet about my career as a writer.

But there is one thing that I do need to say, though I wish I could avoid revealing it. One thing that says something important about my career, but reveals something even more significant about my character. One thing that I've hidden away for years. One thing that I've concealed from others and even from myself. Buried it so deep that for long periods of my life, I've managed almost to erase it from my memory. I began my story by remembering the golden trowel that Mr Potter told his students about. It is a useful metaphor. But sometimes an archaeologist turning over the soil gently with their trowel will come upon something that no one knew was there, something that shouldn't be there, something that needs to be exposed, occasionally even defused, before it destroys everything around it. That's where we are now in my story.

The truth is, *I didn't write that first successful novel.* I should say that again so that you don't miss it. *I didn't write my first successful novel.* That must sound ridiculous. It must make you think that anyone who could pass off someone else's work as his own must be a despicable individual. Sometimes I can't believe it myself. But if I take you through the months that led up to it happening, maybe you can at least understand how it happened, how I could do such a thing.

Before I hook up with Harry Lipman as my agent, I submit my manuscript to a long list of publishers in the hope of publication. Either it's assigned to the notorious 'slush pile' and I never hear back, or there's yet another standard rejection letter in the mail informing me that what I've written is 'not the kind of thing we're looking for'. I begin to despair that my efforts will ever see the light of day. Now let's pick it up from there…

When Harry agrees to take me on back in November 1996, he demands to see printed manuscripts of my efforts rather than just receiving the electronic versions. Harry tells all his writers that he's unashamedly 'old school' and that reading what you've written on a computer screen just won't cut it. You need to get up from your desk, read it aloud from a printed page, he insists, or you'll never know if your writing is any good, never know what it sounds like. So I mail my printed manuscript to him and a week later he invites me to his office to hear his verdict.

'You can write, my boy,' he says, taking off his glasses and wiping them with a large blue handkerchief. 'Oh yes, you can write. You know how to use words alright.'

My spirits lift immediately and just for a moment I allow myself to dream of the glittering career as a novelist that lies ahead of me with such unqualified approval from someone who knows the publishing world as well as he does. But Harry isn't finished. And Harry, as I'm about to discover, doesn't throw out cheap compliments. He waits until I respond with a grateful smile. And only then, when he knows my guard is down, does he deliver the body blow.

'The trouble is, Mr Binnie, I don't believe a word of it. You're in your mid-twenties, but you're still the clever kid at school who knows how to impress people with words. Discerning readers will quickly suss you out. They want more than that kind of fluff. They want you to show them something, something they've always known deep down but never been able to put into words. In short, they want some kind of truth.'

He gets out of his chair, picks up my manuscript, and walks round the desk until he's standing over me.

'So, Mr Alexander Binnie, my boy, take this stuff home and burn it. You can do better. Come back when you've produced something that's worth my time and worthy of your talent.'

To say that I leave his office with my tail between my legs would fail to do justice to how I'm feeling right then. No dog that's been spurned by its master was ever half as miserable as I am on my way home with his words still ringing in my ears.

But two months later I'm back in Harry's office having hand-delivered my printed manuscript the week before. And this time he's genuinely pleased with my offering.

'See, I told you that you could do better. And, my word, you *have* done better. This has got some depth to it. I'm willing to go to war on your behalf for this one. We'll still get some rejections, of course. That pretty much always happens. But this'll get picked up by someone. Rely on me.'

We chat for a few moments more, before we shake hands and I turn to leave, feeling as if I'm walking on air. Just as I reach the door, he calls out to me.

'And you're something of a speed-merchant, I see. To produce a manuscript like this in the time you've had is pretty good going. Well done.'

I mumble my thanks, but I don't turn back. I don't want him to see the flush of embarrassment on my face at his undeserved compliment. I'm not a fast writer and I could never have churned out that kind of work in less than two months. In fact, for weeks after our first meeting, I can't write anything at all. Harry's tongue-lashing, intended to get me writing, has had the opposite effect. For weeks the pages in the notebook where I scribble down ideas to get me started remain empty. For weeks I sit and stare at a blank screen. For weeks nothing happens. Absolutely nothing. And then I remember a box of papers that's been in my possession for a few years now and that I keep meaning to go through. It's the box that was given to me by the widow of Mr Potter after his death. I open it and begin slowly to go through its contents. At first, I'm just looking for some inspiration, maybe some notes made by my old mentor who taught me so much about writing. A hastily written paragraph, perhaps, that might contain some gem that will spark my imagination. Anything that might break through the writer's block I can't get over. Anything that might get the creative juices flowing again.

That's when I find the bundle of closely typed A4 sheets. I remove the thick red rubber band that's holding them together and begin to read through the 200 or so A4 pages. To my astonishment it's the final draft of a novel which obviously was never published. There's no correspondence, no covering letter to accompany the manuscript, no rejection note. Nothing. He wrote all this and never even sent it to a publisher! He's given it the title of *Mr Betteridge's Bicycle*. It's a fictionalised version of his life as a schoolteacher, it's poignant and funny, and *it's very good*. And it makes me realise just how much his writing has influenced mine. The flow of words, the rhythm of his sentences, the way he paints word pictures and brings a scene to life – I learned it all from him. My work is much more like his than I could have imagined – only not quite as good as this.

I keep reading longer than I should before I realise that it's half past one in the morning and it's time I was asleep. I shuffle the pages together again, slip the rubber band back over them, and put them carefully back in the box. I get ready for bed. But I can't sleep. My mind is going over and over what I've just been reading. And a thought is slowly but surely taking shape in my mind. I try to dismiss it. It wouldn't be right, I tell myself. It'd be cheating. But it won't go away.

So I change tack. Instead of trying to resist the idea, I start to rationalise it: Mr Potter's novel is too good to be left lying in a box. He deserves to have it published. But no one is going to be remotely interested in publishing material by a history teacher they've never heard of. A teacher who's been dead for a few years now. I mean, it's hard enough to get a publisher to look at your stuff when you're still alive! Come on, be sensible about this. So... what if I go through it, put my own stamp on it, introduce another character or two, move it to a different location, set it all against a more contemporary backdrop? Surely that's better than leaving it to rot in a box. And I need something to clear the writer's block that's paralysing my mind. I need something to take to Harry Lipman if I don't want to start looking for another agent. I can put a dedication in the front of the book. And it'll be honouring Mr Potter's memory in a way. Won't it? When you look at it like that, there's no valid reason why I shouldn't do it.

And that's what I do. I hand my agent a novel that someone else wrote, with my name on the front page as the author. Of course, I retype it. And it has enough similarities in style to the stuff I've given him earlier that I manage to fool even a reader as experienced as Harry. But apart from a few adjustments, a bit of tinkering here and there, it *isn't* my work. That's why I can't allow myself a backward glance when Harry congratulates me on my ability to produce such great work at such high speed. And that's how my career was built on a lie.

Now, four years into the new millennium, it's turning out to be a more successful career than I dared hope for. *Bald Man on a Squeaky Bike* continues to sell well and to provide me with enough money to buy my own home in Hampstead, give up my job at Pomphrey's Funeral Directors, and devote myself to writing full-time. The publishers gave me a substantial advance on my second novel which allowed me to take my time in writing it. It came out three years ago to popular and critical acclaim. 'Zander Bennings' long-awaited follow-up to *Bald Man on a Squeaky Bike* doesn't disappoint,' was the verdict of one reviewer, while another said equally succinctly, 'This is a tale for our times. Possibly the publishing event of 2001.' Once the round of interviews and personal appearances demanded by the publishers comes to an end, I start work on novel number three and hope to have it ready soon. Success brings rewards other than the money, important as that is. It gives me the freedom to devote myself to writing and opens doors to meet interesting people. But, perhaps best of all, it helps me come to terms with the admittedly unusual conception of my first novel and even begin to feel that this is one case in which the end has justified the means.

chapter 13
matrimonial matters
2004

My father is standing in the doorway, sheltering from the cold March rain and looking impatiently at his watch when our taxi pulls up in front of the registry office and Monica and I get out. We met in October at a dinner party organised by a mutual acquaintance and moved in together just a couple of months ago, so she's understandably a little nervous at meeting my parents for the first time, particularly as this happens to be their wedding day.

From his reaction when he sees us, I suspect that my father is even more apprehensive than she is about this first encounter. His initial irritation at our last-minute arrival has instantly given way to a look of sheer astonishment at the sight of the elegant young woman with the figure of a model – which is indeed her line of work – holding his son's hand and emerging from a hackney cab. Had I been on my own, I'm sure he would have greeted me with a sarcastic comment about my lack of punctuality. On this occasion, however, he ignores me completely and focuses his attention on Monica as he beckons us through the door and into the warmth of the foyer.

'We're really glad that you've come today.' He holds the door open and gives her a kiss on the cheek. 'It's taken Sue and me a long time to get around to making everything legal and respectable. We've been together since 1970, but we've waited until now to officially tie the knot. I guess that's what you call waiting until you're really sure. But for all that, it's a special day for us. Thanks for coming with Alex.'

Like everyone else in my present circle of friends, Monica's only ever known me as Zander and I can see that for a fleeting moment she can't think who Alex is. She quickly catches on, however, and charms my father by telling him, with a degree of exaggeration bordering on untruthfulness, that I've told her so much about him and Mum that she feels as if she knows them already. It's a little white lie, but it's enough to drive away any remaining traces of irritation and put him in a good mood for the rest of the day. My mother is even more overawed when we join her in the reception room. I try to put her at ease as I kiss her on the cheek and introduce her to the elegant woman standing by my side.

'Mum, the is Monica Lonan, my partner. Sorry it's taken so long for you two to meet. But I'm sure you'll like each other.'

Mum smiles nervously and I can see that her attention is focused on the *haute couture* clothes my partner is wearing. I sense immediately from her unease that she's unfavourably comparing her own perfectly appropriate dress, purchased for the occasion from a fairly upmarket high street store, with Monica's ridiculously expensive outfit that comes from one of Italy's most exclusive fashion houses. We engage in the kind of unnatural and stilted conversation that usually prevails in public buildings like this as we wait in the anteroom for the registrar to invite us into the nondescript secular chapel where the formalities are to be carried out.

The ceremony, such as it is, is brief and to the point, just as my parents intended, a purely private act whose sole purpose is to formalise legally what has been true for them for more than thirty years. Something, my father argued, that would provide added protection for Sue if he should die first and some jobsworth official should question her status. Monica and I are the only witnesses and it sounds odd to my ears when they respond to the registrar's request to repeat what he explains are the 'contracting words':

> I call upon – these persons here present – to
> witness that I Alexander Binnie – do take you,
> Susan Ramsey – to be my lawful wedded wife.

I can't help thinking how strange the concept of marriage as a contract would have seemed to my great-grandparents, Sandy and Peggy Binnie, whose marriage had been solemnised in what I imagine would have been the austere and sombre setting of a Presbyterian Scottish kirk at the beginning of the twentieth century. Or of the contrast with the wedding of my grandparents, Alec and Irene Binnie, in that drab period between two world wars when they'd made their vows dressed in their quaint Victorianesque uniforms with a Salvation Army flag held aloft behind them as a colourful reminder that their commitment to be faithful to each other was an extension of their commitment to be faithful to the God in whom they both fervently believed.

And now, in this room where the bland furnishings seem to highlight the loss of a sacred dimension to life and the apparent impossibility of replacing it with a secular equivalent, we are enacting this brief civic rite from which any religious references have been deliberately excluded. The couple being joined in matrimony are not shy young people nervously anticipating an intimacy for which they have saved themselves until this day. These are two people who've already loved and lived with each other for half a lifetime and are pledging their troth thirty-four years after setting up home together. And they are doing so in the presence of another two people – their only child and a glamorous fashion model they have just met for the first time – who have decided to cohabit having known each other for only a couple of months.

It is a moment that encapsulates the tension of which I've been becoming increasingly aware since that morning my grandparents turned up unexpectedly as I was getting ready to leave for my first term at university. I am at one and the same time bound to those past generations by ties of blood, and yet separated from them by so much more than just the passing of the years. I am who I am because of them, and yet I am utterly different from them in so many ways. I am their progeny, and yet here I am in this room, a figure in a bizarre post-religious, twenty-first century tableau that would look to them like a scene from an alien culture.

A sharp dig in the ribs from Monica jolts me back into the moment and I realise that the registrar has declared my parents to be legally married. As we step forward to congratulate them, the strains of a love song come through the speakers discreetly concealed in the wall behind us. My father puts his finger to his lips and makes a hushing sound, and the four of us stand still and listen, without speaking. It is a hymn of a kind, a canticle to a love that makes no reference to a higher authority or a deeper passion.

> O my love is like a red, red rose
> That's newly sprung in June;
> O my love is like the melody
> That's sweetly played in tune.

> So fair art thou, my bonnie lass,
> So deep in love am I;
> And I will love thee still, my dear,
> Till a' the seas gang dry.

> Till a' the seas gang dry, my dear,
> And the rocks melt wi' the sun;
> I will love thee still, my dear,
> While the sands o' life shall run.

When the music fades, I hug my mother and shake my father's hand. I light-heartedly congratulate him on his choice of music, appropriate both to the occasion and to his place of birth, and make a jocular comment about him being an old romantic after all. But the lyrics of the song have brought my mind right back to the train of thought it was following when Monica nudged me just a few minutes ago. Yes, this is a scene that would have seemed odd to earlier generations of the Binnie family. Yes, the world may be different from the one in which my grandparents lived. And yes, my generation and my parents' generation may have drifted a long way from the unquestioned religious certainties to which their lives were anchored. Have we, to our eternal cost, carelessly lost a great treasury of faith? Or have we, to our lasting benefit, courageously liberated ourselves from the confines of a narrow religious outlook on life?

Those are questions to which I have no ready answer. But not everything has changed. What I can never deny and what I understand more clearly every day is our need to love and to be loved, to find security in relationships that are built on mutual respect and buttressed by forgiveness when that respect is damaged by our predisposition to hurt each other. These are the things that will stand the test of time and the vagaries of changing circumstances.

Once again, Monica brings my reflections to an end as she slips her arm into mine and we follow my parents out of the building. There's no chauffeur-driven limousine waiting for us. We make our way to a side street just behind the registrar's office where their car is parked and drive to a nearby restaurant where lunch has been booked. Fortunately for Monica, who doesn't want to walk any distance wearing stiletto heels and a very tight-fitting dress under her even more expensive coat, the wind has dropped and the rain has eased. The improvement in the weather, however, doesn't make it any easier for her to climb into the back of my father's four-by-four with the kind of elegance that women in her profession like to maintain. The bonhomie that she was exuding ten minutes earlier has rapidly turned to a brooding silence. By the time we reach the *Brasserie de Pierre* I'm growing anxious as to how I can manage the situation so that her change of mood doesn't spoil my parents' wedding lunch.

As things transpire, my diplomatic skills are not required. The attentive waiter who greeted us has only just shown us to our table when one of our fellow-diners saunters across from the other side of the restaurant. He's dressed in an apparently casual but carefully coordinated style that immediately tells me he expends a great deal of time and effort to create the impression of not caring about how he looks. From his practised confident air, I hazard a guess that he's employed in advertising or public relations. He's still six feet away from us when he begins to speak and I'm sure that my snap judgement isn't far from the truth. His attention is focused exclusively on the most glamorous member of our party.

'Monica, darling, good to see you again.' He leans across the table and kisses her on both cheeks. 'Tony Randle – you remember me? We worked together last year on the shoot for the toothpaste commercial. You're looking great. How are you?'

My mother is clearly impressed by the scene that's playing out before us. My father is looking at me with an expression that tells me he thinks I was playing well above my league when I won the affections of the woman sat next to me. And Monica, her mood immediately lifted by the flattery being bestowed on her, has suddenly shaken off her irritation at having to walk 100 yards in the rain and clamber into the back seat of a car that clearly wasn't designed with models in mind who need to make a good impression at all times. For the next few minutes, while the three of us listen and wait, she and the photographer

168

indulge in the kind of superficial pleasantries that communicate nothing of any consequence and are never remotely at risk of reaching the level of serious adult conversation. I'm just happy to witness the encounter with the detached fascination and amusement that I often feel when we're out together.

If anyone had told me six months ago that I'd be living with someone like Monica, someone who confesses she hasn't managed to read a book all the way to the end since she left school at the age of sixteen, I'd have laughed at them. But maybe the old saying that 'opposites attract' is right. She does fascinate me. Of course, she's strikingly good-looking. All of my male friends find her physically attractive and I'm certainly no different from them in that respect. But there's more to it than that. There's a childlike naivety in her intellectually unsophisticated approach to life that makes her so different from all my other friends and, most of the time, so easy to be with. I never want to argue with her over big issues in the way I do with other people whom I know well. We can just *be*, be together without some of the things that often complicate adult relationships. But that's only one part of her personality.

Alongside the seeming innocence there's something wild and untamed, even a little dangerous. There are times when she completely ignores the normal conventions of society and behaves just as she pleases. If she decides she really wants something, she'll stop at nothing to get it. And her moods can change in an instant and then change back again just as quickly. When her anger flares up, as it does not infrequently, it spills over those around her with the force of an erupting volcano before it subsides and she dissolves into tears or laughter.

Life with Monica is, not to overstate things, always interesting and unpredictable. And it's a life that at one and the same time, is exhausting and yet addictive. After only a couple of months, I find it difficult to imagine living without her.

Tony, the effusive photographer, having exhausted his hail-fellow-well-met routine and kissed my girlfriend theatrically on both cheeks one more time, returns to his table. But the exchange has left Monica in high spirits and she happily chats with my parents, who find her simplicity and apparent lack of guile charming. To cap it all off, the food at the *Brasserie de Pierre* is excellent and the meal is a great success. I do have my suspicions that Pierre, the proprietor of the establishment, who comes to our table with a bunch of roses to congratulate '*les jeunes amoureux*' on tying the knot, is trying a little too hard with his French accent. He bears a remarkable resemblance to an old friend of my dad's called Peter whose considerably more downmarket restaurant was a favourite of the family when I was in my teens. He's obviously gone up in the culinary world. And, to give him his due, he's definitely mastered the art of Gallic cuisine and hospitality.

As we say goodbye to my folks and get into the taxi to head back to our place in Hampstead, I'm glad that we made the decision not to come by car. The afternoon has gone so well and the atmosphere has been so convivial that I've had several glasses of wine over my usual limit. I'm not drunk, but I'm certainly not in a fit state to drive. I let myself sink into the seat and close my eyes, relieved that our taxi driver is doing the hard work of negotiating his way through the London rush-hour traffic. I become vaguely aware of Monica tapping my arm, but I deliberately don't respond in the hope that she'll give up and let me carry on snoozing. But she keeps tapping and eventually I reluctantly ask her what she wants. I catch her reply, but I'm sure that I must be misunderstanding what she's saying. Too much alcohol in the afternoon, a time I'm not used to drinking, is obviously fuddling my brain and playing tricks with my hearing. I begin to drift back to sleep. But she says it again, only this time louder and more slowly.

'Zander, I think we should get married.'

Now I'm awake, sitting upright, my eyes wide open in disbelief. I'd put what she's saying down to the effects of what she's been drinking, but she never over-imbibes and I doubt she's had more than half a glass of wine.

'You think what?' I ask, leaning forward and making sure that the glass partition in front of us is closed. This isn't a conversation that I want a London cab driver to overhear.

'Don't pretend you don't know what I said.' Monica is stone-cold sober and deadly serious. 'I really enjoyed meeting your mum and dad today. You've been really lucky. My folks split up before I was three. My mum brought me up on her own. I never knew my dad.'

'You're right. I guess I have been lucky. But what's that got to do with us getting married? Things are OK as they are. And it's taken my mum and dad thirty-odd years to get round to doing it. We'll think about it, if you want. That's a promise. But there's no hurry.'

I hope that'll be enough to keep her happy and I can drop off to sleep again. Maybe she'll forget all about it by the time we get home. But it's a forlorn hope. No sooner have we got out of the taxi and stepped inside the front door than she picks up where she'd left off.

'Zander, I know you're trying to avoid the subject. You told me that you loved me when you asked me to live with you. Why don't you want to talk about getting married? Are you beginning to wish we hadn't moved in together? Is there somebody else?'

'Of course there isn't anybody else.' I pull her into my arms and hold her very tightly. 'It's just that this is taking me by surprise. I'd no idea you felt like this. I thought that we both saw marriage as an outdated institution. Just a piece of paper that doesn't make any difference to how we feel about each other. I promise you we'll talk about it tomorrow. Please?'

She mumbles her half-hearted agreement and we call a truce for the rest of the day. The atmosphere is frosty, though it does begin to thaw a little as the evening wears on. And, by the time we go to bed, she seems much happier. I'm relieved at the change in her mood and I drift off to sleep hoping that something else will take her attention in the morning.

Monica isn't normally an early riser and it usually takes her well over an hour to wake up, shower, and perform the 101 beauty-enhancing procedures that allow her to face the day feeling that she's done everything to look her best. But next morning, to my surprise, she's awake before me. When I wander into the kitchen in my pyjamas, she's not only dressed and looking her best, but breakfast's been prepared and the table's set. It's nothing more elaborate than a bowl of cereal followed by toast and marmalade and a pot of coffee, but it's the first time this has happened since we set up home together.

At first, I can't think why she's gone to all this trouble. Then I remember yesterday's conversation. I'm not sure how to deal with this, so I turn on the radio, making the excuse that I want to hear the news headlines. She knows I'm stalling for time and she's content to wait for me to finish before she speaks. I switch the radio off and try to prepare for what she's about to say.

'You promised me we could talk about it today. I said my bit yesterday. So I'd like to hear what you've got to say now that you've had a chance to sleep on it.'

I smile obligingly and skirt around the subject for the next five minutes, trying to offer some practical reasons why this isn't the right time for us to consider marriage. We need time to get to know each other, I tell her. I'm working on a book that's taking up all my attention. She's got her career to think of. It'll take time to plan for a wedding. But it's basically an exercise in delaying tactics, an approach which does nothing to dissuade Monica from the course on which she's clearly set her mind. She waits for the right moment and then she does something that's always her trump card when she wants something badly. She begins to cry.

'What you really mean, Zander,' she says, allowing the tears to roll down her face and smudge her mascara, 'is that you don't really love me. This whole thing has just been a way of getting me into bed. And now you've had what you wanted, you're getting fed up with me. You want to find a way out...'

I'm suddenly afraid that she's going to walk out on me. Whether what I'm feeling right now is love, I'm not sure. But I do know that the prospect of not having her in my life isn't one that I want to contemplate. Without really thinking about what I'm doing, I push my chair back, walk round the table and kneel in front of her.

'Of course I don't want to find a way out. And I certainly don't want you to leave.' I take hold of her hand and look up at her face. 'Monica Lonan, will you marry me please?'

But I can see that she's not about to be taken in by what she suspects is a bit of play-acting. She wants to make absolutely certain of victory, to be doubly sure that there's no way I can wriggle out of this.

'Now you're just making fun of me. That's unkind. All my life people who've told me they loved me have abandoned me. I can't face that happening again.'

Now the tears are really flowing and the lines running down her carefully applied make-up remind me of the sad clown in a circus act. The rational part of my mind is trying to tell me that I'm being manipulated, played like a sentimental tune on an old violin. But I don't want to listen to that voice. All I know is that I am besotted with this woman.

'Don't be silly.' I reach up and cup her face in my hands, which makes her look more vulnerable and appealing to me than ever. 'I love you. You're right. We should get married. You mean the world to me.'

I pick a napkin off the table and dry her eyes. I can feel her body beginning to relax. The tears slowly subside.

'So, I'm asking you again. Monica Lonan, will you be my wife?'

That does it. She leans forward, hugs me, and tells me she loves me more than anything in the world. She knows and I know that I've capitulated. What I don't know is that she's about to press home her advantage.

'And, Zander, can we do it properly, please?'

I can't quite figure out exactly what she means by her question, but I decide I've done the romantic thing and I've been on my knees long enough. I stand up, go back to my place at the other side of the table and nod in agreement. I assure her that we'll book a posh restaurant and invite whoever she thinks should be there.

'No, that's not what I mean,' she says in an untypically demure voice and with a beatific smile that I've never seen on her face before. 'I mean, can we have a church wedding? It's much nicer. I can understand why your parents would be happy with a ceremony in a registry office. But it's not the same as a church…'

She looks at me with the pitiful expression of a child who's being denied the only thing she's ever wanted.

'Zander, I've always wanted to walk up the aisle to be married. Please…'

I'm totally unprepared for this. She's not content with winning. She doesn't just want to get married. She wants to walk up the aisle of a church. *That's a victory procession!* I protest that we're not religious, that we never go to church, that it would be a meaningless charade, that arranging it would be a hassle we don't need. But Monica is not the kind of girl to be dissuaded from something that she's set her heart on. She reminds me of the stories I've told her about my family history, about the weddings of Sandy Binnie and Alec Binnie. A church wedding, she argues, would simply be continuing the family tradition, a link with the past. I can see that this is another argument that I'm not going to win.

'Well, if that's what you really want,' I say grudgingly, 'we'll get married in a church.'

I smile meekly and concede defeat. There's no reason for me to be unduly concerned about what I've just agreed to. It's only what any decent man would do. All that's happened is that I've put my own preferences on one side to indulge the woman I love, a woman who wants the trappings of a church wedding. But I can't quite dismiss the feeling that something has shifted in my relationship with Monica.

chapter 14
conversations with a clergyman
2004

The days that follow are just the first stirrings of what rapidly becomes a whirlwind of activity for Monica as she scours the internet and adds to the growing mountain of glossy catalogues that drop through the letterbox almost every day, all of them advertising everything that's required, and a thousand and one other things that I can't imagine any couple ever needing, for the perfect wedding. But my bride-to-be possesses a laser-like focus that can cut through all this information and home in on exactly what she wants. My part is just to pay the bills and find the right church at which to stage these perfect nuptials on which she's set her heart.

She's happy to leave the first of those tasks entirely in my hands with absolutely no interference from her. With regard to the second, however, she sets down strict parameters within which I need to work. These relate not to the beliefs or practices of the church, things in which Monica has little interest. 'Well, they all believe in God, so they're pretty much all the same, aren't they?' she reasons. No, her concerns relate entirely to the aesthetics and trappings of the venue. *Will the vicar wear those robes that look so splendid? Does it have an organ that will sound really impressive playing the 'Wedding March' when I walk up the aisle? Are there suitable backgrounds in front of which we can stage our photographs?*

Paying the bills for Monica's expensive choices proves to be an ongoing chore that lasts for several months, but sorting out the church is solved much quicker than I anticipate. A week after our conversation, I'm driving past St Mark's which is no more than five minutes from our cottage in Hampstead and stands where the village borders on the Heath. I've never paid much attention to it before, other than noticing that it's an impressive building in a picturesque setting. Now it occurs to me that here's a church right on our doorstep that's exactly what we're looking for.

I park the car and decide to take a look around. At first, I intend to walk around the exterior and check that there's nothing just out of view that might spoil those all-important wedding photos. I pause at the gate and read the gold lettering on the freshly painted royal-blue noticeboard. It gives the times of the services and assures me that, like everyone else who passes this way, I'm welcome just to wander in at any time of the day and take a moment to pray or simply to sit in quietness. I've no urge to pray and I don't feel any particular need for quietness right now. But, if the place is open, I might as well have a look inside. Then I can give Monica a full report on its suitability for our impending nuptials.

I walk up the path and push open the heavy studded door. Immediately I'm greeted with that musty, woody smell that always gives old churches a feeling of timelessness. My father, who's been in so many places like this in the line of duty, calls it 'the odour of sanctity' and confesses that he always associates it with death and bereavement. I slip quietly into the pew nearest the entrance. The sun is shining through the stained-glass window at the far end of the building, projecting colourful patterns onto the floor around the altar. I'm not close enough to make out all the details, and I probably wouldn't understand the full import of what is depicted if I were standing right underneath. But, even for an agnostic like me who's sceptical of talk about 'a spiritual realm' and untutored in the symbolism of ecclesiastical art, it has a powerful effect at a level deeper than my conscious mind. I neither know nor care what the artist intended, but I do know how it makes me feel: like something is breaking through, speaking to me wordlessly from a depth of which I'm usually unaware. If I ever do decide I need to pray, this would be the kind of place I'd probably come to, even though I'm not sure if there would be anybody listening.

Then I remember why I'm here and all I've still got to do before the end of the day. I ease myself out of the pew and saunter up the aisle with my hands in my pockets, glancing this way and that, surveying the place with the eye of a man who's been commissioned to find a suitable venue for a fairy-tale wedding. And this sixteenth-century church really is the perfect setting for Monica's special day – the stillness that makes you feel as if you've entered another world, the stone flags on the floor, the dark wood of the pews, the organ pipes glinting in the sunlight, the pillars hung with bright, colourful banners. The only thing that's needed to complete the picture she has in her imagination is a vicar dressed in robes standing in front of me. Right on cue, a clergyman appears from a side door. But far from being garbed in ecclesiastical finery, he's wearing nothing more elaborate than jeans, a pair of natty red trainers, and a grey crewneck sweater that leaves just enough of his dog collar showing to identify him as a man of the cloth. He smiles as he approaches me.

'You look as if you're really appreciating our building. It is rather special, isn't it? Still takes my breath away.' His smile broadens. 'Very different from the 1970s building on an inner-city estate where I was the vicar until twelve months ago.'

Encouraged by his friendly manner and the fact that he doesn't seem in any great rush to get to wherever he's going, I tell him the reason for my visit, explaining that though we live in his parish, we've no strong religious convictions and no real links with any place of worship. When I ask a little awkwardly if there would be any conditions to being married in his church, he invites me to sit beside him on the front pew while he answers my question.

'Well, you wouldn't expect me to say anything other than that we'd love to welcome you to any of our services at St Mark's.' He smiles again, something he seems to do frequently and with disarming ease. 'But no, we don't impose any conditions or force people to attend services. It's enough for me that people want to seek God's blessing on their union. I'd want to meet with you and your partner, talk things through, make sure you're both at ease with the vows you'd be making in what would, of course, be a Christian marriage ceremony. And we do offer marriage preparation courses four times a year if you'd be interested in attending one of those.'

He introduces himself as Alan Kibbell, known to his friends, he tells me, as 'Al', to most of his flock as 'The Rev', and only to the more staid members of the congregation as 'Vicar'. When I respond by telling him that I'm Zander Bennings, he recognises my name, raises his eyebrows to signal that he's impressed, and makes suitably complimentary comments about my books, all of which, he assures me, he and his wife have read and enjoyed. I try to look suitably modest, thank him for his time and agree to his suggestion that I make an appointment with his secretary in the church office for Monica and me to meet with him in the next month. We've just shaken hands and I'm turning to leave when he stops me.

'Forgive me if I'm wrong, and feel free to tell me to mind my own business. But I think we've met before, though it must be twelve or thirteen years or so since I last saw you. I've been trying to work out why you looked so familiar since I saw you walking up the aisle. It was only when you told me you were Zander Bennings, the writer, that it came back to me. I guess it's the similarity in the names. We were only nodding acquaintances back then and I didn't mix in the same circles as you, so you won't remember me. But am I right in thinking that your name was originally Alex Binnie and you read English at Oxford? Graduated in '92?'

I acknowledge that he's right. Zander Bennings and Alex Binnie are indeed one and the same. And, yes, now that he mentions it, I do vaguely remember his name from university days. Definitely a coincidence, I agree, that we should meet up again like this. But certainly a happy coincidence, given that he's just agreed to conduct my wedding. He has more to tell me.

'The odd thing is that in a funny kind of way, you're partly responsible for where I am and what I'm doing with my life today. You and your friend Byron to be precise.'

My wide-eyed expression of surprise at this remark makes him laugh even more than he's done already. But I can tell by his voice when he begins speaking again that he's not joking.

'No, I'm being serious. I'd seen you two holding court one evening in a bar. To be honest, I wasn't impressed. I was a very earnest young man back then. I'd had a very powerful conversion experience the year before I went up to Oxford that really changed me. I had all the zeal of a new convert and a giant dose of intolerance towards those who didn't share my convictions. Byron's camp, comic persona definitely didn't meet with my approval.'

He shakes his head and lets out a long sigh. There was an expression of genuine regret on his face.

'I was pretty outspoken in my criticism and when word got around that he was HIV positive and had AIDS I didn't have much sympathy. When I heard that he'd died I'm sorry to say that I took the line that was still all too common back then, that this was God's judgement. But as time passed and I came to understand my faith more deeply, I had a real change of heart. I mean, if God sent plagues on everyone who veered from the true path, there'd be nobody left on this planet. And why would he send a sickness on one group of people and let the rest of us off scot-free? That didn't make any sense when I thought about it.'

He pauses and allows himself to smile again, before clasping his hands under his chin and taking a deep breath.

'Then, of course, you came back to Oxford at the start of our second year. I could see the effect his death had had on you. And I heard about how you'd been with him when he died. Long story short, it all helped me understand that my faith has to be much more about caring about people than judging them. And that was really the initial impetus for me putting myself forward for ordination. There were several times when I would see you around and think that I ought to speak to you. But… I dunno… probably a mixture of shyness and embarrassment about how I'd reacted in the past kept me from approaching you. And now you turn up in my church asking me to marry you and I discover you're living in my parish! What's going on here?'

'Well, I'm not sure what's going on either,' I respond, as we shake hands one more time and get ready to part. 'I do know that I've been accused of a lot of things over the years, but never of encouraging anyone to sign up to be an Anglican vicar.'

That evening I report my findings to a tired but delighted Monica who's just come home from yet another shopping spree. I've never known her eager to get to church, our only previous visits having been to attend a couple of christenings of friends' babies. But by eleven o'clock the following morning, at her insistence, we're sitting in St Mark's together appraising all we can see and she agrees that this is just the venue she's been hoping for. She's so keen to buy into the entire package that not only do we meet with Alan Kibbell a week later to talk through the vows, but we also sign up to attend one of the marriage preparation days he mentioned.

It proves to be an interesting experience. Monica is happy just to be there and she chats enthusiastically with the other four couples who've accepted the invitation to attend the event. I find that the part of the day devoted to making sure you really know each other and have a proper understanding of the challenges of spending a lifetime together causes me to feel a little concerned. On the way home, I wonder aloud if we're really ready to take this step and I tentatively suggest that maybe it would make sense to wait a little longer before we tie the knot. But Monica looks at me with the pouting face of a disappointed child. It's an expression she knows I can never resist. Why would two people who love each other as much as we do want to wait any longer, she asks me. There's just the hint of a tear in her eye as she says my suggestion makes her think that maybe I don't love her. The conversation ends with me assuring her that I do love her and that we won't delay a day longer than it takes to get everything arranged for the big day.

On the afternoon of 5th November 2004, with my agent, Harry Lipman, as my best man and Monica's older sister as her bridesmaid, we're married in St Mark's Church by the Reverend Alan Kibbell. The ceremony, which I find surprisingly moving, is dignified and simple. The reception afterwards, which, unsurprisingly, I find exhausting, is anything but. Our fifty guests are ferried to an exclusive hotel on the outskirts of London and treated to a meal that consists of more courses than I can count. I glance at my parents as we're working our way through the cheese course towards the end of this culinary marathon and I can see what they're thinking: this definitely puts their meal at the *Brasserie de Pierre* in the shade.

Before the evening's celebrations get properly under way, everyone is ushered out to the grounds of the hotel to witness a fireworks display, accompanied by Handel's 'Music for the Royal Fireworks' played through the public address system. Impressive as this is to our guests, it represents my one success in limiting the budget for the day. I managed to convince Monica, only after much persuasion, that a recording would be every bit as impressive and considerably less expensive than hiring a small orchestra. When the pyrotechnics have finished, we go back indoors and dance the night away.

It's after one o'clock in the morning when the guests start to drift off and this major production finally comes to an end. Harry Lipman is the last to leave, and typically he has the last word.

'Zander, my boy, that was an occasion and a half. Only a writer with an agent as good as me could afford to stage such an epic.' He pulls me aside, making sure that we're out of earshot of Monica and whispers in my ear. 'Just be careful. Even I can't promise to get you the kind of advances on your books that'll let you maintain that kind of lifestyle for too long.'

The following morning, we fly out to honeymoon in a beach resort in Jamaica. The weather is warm and sunny and Monica is as happy as a child who's been let out of school to spend a holiday at the seaside with her favourite grown-up relative. In a sense, that really is what all this means to her.

Several times in that week I wake early in the morning to the sound of the waves rolling onto the sand just a few feet from our open window. I look at her lying asleep beside me, her breathing quiet and rhythmic, her long dark hair falling over her pillow, her face even more beautiful to me without the make-up she applies with such meticulous care every day. At times like this, I understand who she is and that her need for the expensive and the extravagant is not simply selfishness as some might think. Nor is it just a young woman's taste for glamour and romance. There is a vulnerability in her unconscious expression that reveals all too clearly what her naïve comments in her waking hours so often betray. The lifestyle she craves is a way of compensating for everything she was deprived of in childhood. It gives her a sense that she's someone of value, someone worth loving, someone who deserves to be noticed. I know there are dangers in such emotional fragility in an adult. But those are the moments when I realise more than ever the strength of the attraction that draws me irresistibly to this child-woman.

We come back to the cold and rain of England after a week in the Caribbean sun. Monica has some modelling work that keeps her busy and I try to settle back in to the daily routine of writing. I always find it difficult to motivate myself after a break, but this time, despite knowing that I have a deadline looming early in the new year, my usual initial sluggishness is compounded by a deep unease that won't leave me alone and hinders my concentration. I can't shake off what I tell myself is just an inevitable emotional come-down after the highs of recent events.

Harry Lipman's words at the end of our wedding keep running through my mind and I wonder if my disquiet is down to some kind of guilt about the amount of money we've just spent. I try to dismiss that thought by reminding myself that any man worth his salt always wants to go the extra mile to make sure that his wife is happy on their wedding day. My attempts to reason my way out of my despondency are to no avail, however, and I begin to think about talking to Alan Kibbell about how I'm feeling. We've got to know him quite well over the past few months and he's easy to talk to. He might be able to give me some perspective on things. I decide to wait until after Christmas before I do anything, just to see if my mood begins to lift. But by the end of the festive season, if anything I feel worse and I decide to make the call.

Alan suggests that I come to his vicarage early in January. It's less formal than meeting at the church office, he says. And it's easier to chat without being disturbed by someone calling on church business. I hear myself telling him things I've been trying to avoid, things I haven't fully articulated until now: the growing tension of being at one and the same time bound to the generations of my family who've gone before me and yet feeling increasingly disconnected from them; the gnawing sense of guilt for which I can find no comfort; the ever-present yearnings to find a source of strength that will enable me to live a life that deserves to be called good. He listens to my rambling attempts to explain my disquiet without interrupting, limiting himself to an occasional nod of agreement or a questioning look. I'm half-expecting – to be truthful, I'm dreading – that he'll ask to pray with me or quote me something from the Bible that will either compound my confusion or leave me with an impossibly spiritual and thoroughly impracticable answer. He does neither of those things, but suggests that since it's a crisp, clear day, we take a walk over the Heath. Walking in the fresh air, he says with a characteristic smile, isn't exactly the same as hearing directly from God. But it is in his experience definitely the next best thing.

We stride out briskly for half an hour, confining our conversation to generalities, until we reach the north end of the Heath and sit down on one of the benches in front of Kenwood House. The white walls of the solid seventeenth-century stately home shut off the noise of any traffic passing along the road. There are not many people around and it feels like we have this moment all to ourselves. The air is still, with only the faintest whisper of a breeze, and the view across the lush, green lawns that sweep down to the sparkling water of the lake seems to exist just for us. I'm grateful to be in this place at this time with this man who's willing to listen to me. Alan continues to look straight ahead towards the lake as he begins to speak, his voice so quiet that I have to strain slightly to hear what he's saying.

'You know, Zander, the more I get to know people – I mean, *really* get to know them, spend time with them and listen to them – the more I'm discovering that when they begin to feel something's not quite right with their life, their first impulse is to try to work things out and put things right. And there's certainly a time for doing that. But if you're not careful, you can end up on a treadmill that's hard to get off and leaves you even more exhausted and confused than you were at the start.'

He pauses to allow a solitary jogger to run past us and waits for the sound of his footsteps to fade in the distance before he turns towards me.

'There are two kinds of people in my congregation. There are some who've got it all worked out in their own minds and are convinced that they've put everything right. They've got everything sorted. Or so they think. But they're increasingly in the minority and they're the ones who give me most trouble. The ones I can help the most – and, oddly enough, they're the ones who help *me* the most – are the folk who know they *haven't* got it all worked out and who've realised that they *can't* manage to put it all right. They come because they know they need to hear some good news about how they can do better. They come because they're desperate enough to make a U-turn from how they've been living and find a new path in life. Having listened to you talking about your grandparents and your family history, and knowing you're a man who spends his days looking for the right words, I'm sure you don't need me to tell you what the right word for this is.'

I wait for the killer sentence that will drive home the point he wants to make and tell me exactly what he thinks I should do next. It never comes. Alan gets up and suggests that it's time for us to turn around right now.

'Conversation in the open air on a sunny day is always good. But what matters, Zander, is what we decide to do when the talking stops.'

He immediately begins to stride out in the direction of home. I hesitate for just a moment and then decide I'd better follow.

chapter 15
good deeds and better days
2005–07

It's 12th January, the day after my conversation with Alan. Monica, who has to be up early for a fashion shoot in the morning, has gone to bed, and I'm watching the ten o'clock news on television. It's the usual hodgepodge of information and speculation. Besides all the goings-on in national politics, it ranges from the serious to the ludicrous. As a result of the recent wintry weather there's severe flooding in the north of England, and a ship has run aground off the coast of Scotland with passengers unable to be lifted off because of stormy seas. At the opposite extreme, almost two minutes are given over to a report on the protests from earnest-looking people who are offended to the point of apoplexy by a highly irreverent musical in London's West End that contains a great deal of profane language and features a troupe of tap-dancing members of the Ku Klux Klan.

But it's the last item on the bulletin that captures my attention. It features the unveiling of a sculpture in Manchester earlier in the day that was commissioned to commemorate the Commonwealth Games that were held in the city back in 2002. It is, to say the least, an extraordinary and arresting sight. Made of what looks like rusty old iron, it weighs 165 tonnes, stands 184 feet tall and leans at a crazy angle of 30 degrees, seeming to defy gravity. The most eye-catching thing about this remarkable structure are the 180 spikes that spread out from the supporting legs, like an explosion of corroded metal, seventy-two feet above the ground. They are, the reporter states with what seems like a threatening understatement, 'designed to sway menacingly in the wind'. This bizarre creation has an equally odd name – the '*B of the Bang*'. Normally attention would be focused on the sculptor who's created such an unusual piece of public art. In this instance, however, most of the interest is being directed towards the man who inspired not only its creation, but also its curious title. It's a quotation from the sprinter Linford Christie, who explains his remarkable speed off the blocks by saying that he starts to run, not at the bang of the starter's pistol, but 'at the B of the Bang'.

Other than being vaguely aware of his prowess on the athletics track, I don't know anything about Mr Christie. I assume that he makes no claim to be either a writer or a philosopher. His ability to communicate may be both untutored and unusual, but it certainly enables him to say something that gets to the heart of the matter with the minimum of words. I spend my life trying to use the English language to effect, but I couldn't have come up with anything better than this – the 'B of the Bang'. 'I don't hang around,' he's telling us. 'I start to run at the first possible moment.' I can't help thinking that there's some sound advice here for me that's particularly relevant to my situation at this very moment. What matters, Alan told me yesterday, is what you do when the talking stops. And now – right now – is the time for me to do something. Now is the time to make that U-turn.

I switch off the television, tiptoe quietly through to my study so as not to wake Monica, and take a blank sheet of paper and a pen. At the top of the page I write in bold capitals:

THE B OF THE BANG – FIRST STEPS IN A NEW DIRECTION.

Then I make a brief list:

1. Stop worrying about whether I jumped into this marriage too quickly and start making it work.
2. Set up a charitable trust to use a proportion of my money to benefit others who are less fortunate.
3. Make weekly contact with my parents.
4. Be alert to opportunities that arise to do some good even it inconveniences me.

That's it. Nothing more elaborate than that. I read it over a few times, fold the sheet of paper up and slip it into a drawer in my desk. That night I sleep better than I have done for weeks.

Monica has gone by the time I wake in the morning, though I have a vague memory of her kissing me goodbye and hearing the sound of the chauffeur-driven car door slamming outside the bedroom window as she left for the studio. She won't be back until late in the evening and I'm looking forward to a blissful eight hours of uninterrupted writing. I follow my usual routine for days like this – twenty minutes of exercise to loosen up, finish off my shower with the dial turned to cold to make sure I'm fully awake, and breakfast with a bowl of fruit and a cup of strong coffee while listening to the news headlines on the radio to get my brain ticking over. When I sit down at my desk at precisely five minutes past nine, I know I've got a whole day ahead of me to work, a really productive day. And then the phone rings.

'Alex, sorry to disturb you. It's your old man. Hope it's not one of your writing days.'

He needn't have gone to the trouble of identifying himself. Even though there was some interference on the line that made it difficult to recognise the caller's voice immediately, I knew it had to be him. He and my mum are the only people who still call me Alex.

'Hi Dad. It *is* one of my writing days. It's what I do for a living, in case you'd forgotten.' I realise a little too late that I'm already in danger of forgetting one of the resolutions I made last night. So I make an effort to sound a little less irritated. 'But that's alright. You don't usually call in the morning. Nothing wrong with you or Mum, I hope.'

'Oh no, nothing like that. We're both fine. But I had a call from a woman called Janet Staines. She's a single lady, the sister of Mrs Potter, your old teacher's wife. She's the one that Mrs Potter and Amy went to live with when her husband died. It was really you that she wanted to talk to but she didn't know your number. So I told her that I'd pass on her message. I didn't commit you to anything.'

'Yes, I know Janet,' I reply, still struggling to overcome my annoyance at having what promised to be a perfect writing day interrupted. 'I've visited Mrs Potter and Amy at her house a couple of times since they moved down to live with her. What did she want?'

The message was brief and to the point. Mrs Potter had terminal cancer and had come home from hospital with only a few days to live. But she wanted to speak with me. Her sister had been nervous of making the call, but Mrs Potter had been so insistent that she'd acquiesced to her wishes.

I'm about to tell him that I can't do anything today but that I'll try to get down later in the week. Then I remember the 'B of the Bang' and the last thing on the list I made last night before going to bed: 'Be alert to opportunities that arise to do some good even it inconveniences me'!

An hour later, on a windy day that tugs at the car and makes me think it would have been more sensible to have stayed at home, I'm turning off the M25 onto the M3 and heading into the rain and in the direction of the south coast. By half past one I've reached my destination and I'm parking the car outside number 25 in a row of solid but unpretentious 1930s red-brick terraced houses in Poole. The lace curtain that twitches at the window is a sure sign that the occupants of this particular dwelling are older and longer-established residents than the young couples and first-time buyers who make up the majority of their neighbours and who favour trendy wooden shutters.

Janet has been looking out for my arrival and opens the door before I can ring the bell. She thanks me profusely for coming so quickly and takes me straight into the lounge. It's been converted to a bedroom since my last visit and Mrs Potter is lying in bed propped up by several pillows. Her breathing is laboured, but she's conscious and aware of what's going on around her. Amy is in her wheelchair by the window. They're both obviously glad that I've come, and when I see the expressions on their faces, I'm glad that I overcame my initial reluctance and decided to brave the elements. We chat about the weather and the traffic for five minutes before Janet suggests to Amy that it's time for her nap and takes her out of the room.

I pull a chair up to the side of the bed and Mrs Potter reaches out to take hold of my hand. The firmness of her grip takes me by surprise.

'Thank you for coming. I'm really grateful.' Her struggle to breathe is making it difficult for her to speak and I have to lean close to her to catch her words. 'I don't know who else I could ask.'

I nod and assure her that I'll be happy to do whatever I can to be of help.

'I knew you'd say that. Bill always thought the world of you. He used to say that there was more to you than you realised yourself.' I feel her pull on my hand as she beckons me to come closer still. 'It's Amy. I'm worried about her. My sister's a few years older than I am. She's great with Amy. I don't know how I'd have coped without her. But she's not getting any younger herself. It's really getting too much for her and she's not going to be able to look after my daughter indefinitely.'

She coughs as she tries to clear her throat and I reach for a tissue from the table by the side of the bed to wipe her mouth. I feel her hand squeezing mine a little tighter in an expression of gratitude for this simple act of kindness. It takes a moment or two before her breathing settles enough for her to be able to speak again.

'We were able to put a bit of money aside from the sale of the house when we moved down here but we've had to plough a lot of that into repairs on this place. There's still a few thousand pounds left but it isn't going to be enough to cover the cost of Amy's care. The doctor says that for all her disabilities, she's strong enough to live another ten years. And I don't want her to end up in a place where nobody really knows her. I shouldn't have left it so late, but my cancer was diagnosed just a couple of months ago and the hospital didn't expect it to progress as quickly as it has done. I feel bad about asking you, but I wondered if there was anything you could do to help.'

Exhausted by the effort of speaking, she lets herself relax into the pillow and closes her eyes. Her grip on my hand slowly loosens and I'm not sure if she's asleep or if she's lost consciousness. But I want her to know that her plea hasn't been in vain. I keep hold of her hand and whisper in her ear.

'Don't worry. I promise you that I'll make sure that Amy is well cared for. You can leave all that to me.'

It may be my imagination, but I think she's just squeezed my hand again in acknowledgement of my words. I stay by her bedside, still keeping my hand in hers, but apart from the rise and fall of her chest as she fights for breath, she makes no other sound or movement.

The clock on the mantelpiece strikes two o'clock as I get up and slip quietly out of the room. Janet has made a late lunch, knowing that I haven't eaten since breakfast. As we sit at the table together, I tell her not to worry about the future and that I'll make sure her niece is well cared for. The look of relief on her face is even more eloquent than her effusive words of thanks.

Just as I'm getting ready to leave, Amy wakes up and wants to talk to me. She knows her mother's not well, and though she doesn't fully comprehend how serious her illness is, she understands enough to be worried about what it might mean.

'Mummy says that she's sure you'll help us.' She looks at me with the wide, pleading eyes of a child. 'I hope you can help to make her better.'

I'm thankful when Janet puts her hand on my arm and takes control of the conversation. It relieves me of the burden of finding the words to reply to such an appeal.

'Your mummy's right, Amy. Mr Bennings is going to help us. You don't need to worry. And you know what Mummy told you. God's looking after her and we've got to keep saying our prayers and making sure she's comfortable while she's poorly.'

That seems to satisfy Amy who smiles and insists on giving me a wet, sloppy kiss. I respond with what I hope is a sympathetic and reassuring smile and resist the temptation to take out my handkerchief and wipe the saliva from my face. Janet and I look at each other and wonder how this childlike disabled woman in her fifties will cope with the inevitable loss of her mother.

The journey back to London is slow. Intentionally so. I pull off the road several times, telling myself that that I need a cup of coffee or a loo break. But really, I'm stopping because I need to take my hands off the wheel and my eyes off the road and just sort out my thoughts. Or, more accurately, it's because I need to figure out exactly what it is that I'm feeling right now.

At first, I'm pretty sure that it's simply the sense of satisfaction that every decent human being experiences when we know that we've done the right thing, inconvenienced ourselves to help someone else, shown kindness to someone in need. But I know it's more than that. The further I get on the way home, the more I realise that what I'm feeling is a growing sense of relief. It's as if I can now open a door that I've had to keep locked for too many years. I can turn the key, walk into the room, switch on the light and face the thing that I've had to keep hidden from view. The thing that's like a virus that could prove deadly if I once allowed myself to handle it or breathe the very air that surrounds it. But now it's as if I've just donned a suit of protective clothing that will keep me safe from its power to infect or even destroy me.

You know what the thing that I've had to lock away is. *It's the truth about my first novel – Bald Man on a Squeaky Bike.* It's the manuscript I found, held together by a thick red rubber band. The manuscript that Mr Potter wrote and did nothing with. His novel that was never published. The novel that I've adapted. Adopted as my own. Use whatever word you want. But, please, please, not the word used by the faceless figure who enters my troubled dreams on some nights and causes me to wake with a throbbing in my chest and a knot in my stomach. Not *that* word. Adapted, adopted, borrowed, revised – those are acceptable words for what I've done. But not that word. Not *stolen.* That's not fair. That's going too far. You can't steal from the dead. You can't describe something you've found and put to good use as having been *stolen.* And now I can face the truth without it polluting me. What I did was for the best. I know that now. I know it because my success and the money it's brought means that I'll be able to make sure that Amy Potter will be looked after as long as she lives. I know it because what I've done with her father's novel has given me the resources to care for his disabled daughter. The origins of my first novel may be... how can I put it? Well, somewhat unusual, even a shade unethical if you want to be legalistic about it. But life and its choices are too complex and nuanced to be examined in such a forensic manner. And what I've just committed myself to doing – looking after Amy – surely exempts me from legal scrutiny and protects me from moral judgement for what I once did. So, we can close that door again. Put the thing back under lock and key where it has no power to harm me any longer. I can even forget that it's there and get on with the rest of my life. There's no good reason to open the door and show it to others. That would serve no purpose.

On the last of my stops, about twenty miles from Hampstead, I get a text message from Monica, telling me that she won't be home until eight o'clock, and asking me to get some takeaway food. I call and order her favourite meal from her favourite Italian restaurant in the village, remembering to include a bottle of their best Prosecco, the one alcoholic drink she actually enjoys.

By the time she gets home, I've put on some romantic music, lit several candles and laid the table, complete with napkins and the best cutlery set out in the proper order. As soon as she steps through the door, I'm ready to serve the food which has been keeping warm in the oven. She's suitably impressed and, knowing my lack of domestic skills, she's pleasantly surprised by this unprecedented attention to the etiquette of fine dining on my part.

When we've finished eating and I've cleared the table, she asks me how my writing has gone today. I'm about to tell her what's happened and how my plans had to be changed, until I remember to do the gentlemanly thing and invite her to talk about her day first. She's even more surprised at my unusually gallant behaviour, but she willingly takes the next fifteen minutes to give me a rundown on what it's like to be the centre of attention at a fashion photoshoot. But even Monica, who never has any problem talking about herself and her work, reaches the end of all she has to say. What's more, she's beginning to show tell-tale signs that she's growing suspicious of my unusually gentlemanly behaviour. Her eyes narrow a little as she curls her legs underneath her on the couch and tells me that she really does want to hear about my day.

'Well, I've driven down to Dorset and back. To Poole, to be exact. Got home just half an hour or so before you did.' I see an opportunity to add to the points I've already scored for my good deeds in the last hour. So, trying to sound as casual as I can, I add: 'Then I dashed around the kitchen making sure everything was right for our romantic dinner.'

It's been an evening of surprises for Monica and this latest revelation leaves her completely baffled.

'What on earth were you doing in Poole on a day like this?' she asks, looking at me suspiciously. 'You told me you had to get a full day's writing done.'

I take a moment to make sure she's sitting comfortably before I launch into my tale. She's interested and sympathetic, nodding and making all the right 'oohs' and 'aahs' at the appropriate places in the story. It's only when I get to the point where I need to tell her about my decision to provide for Amy's future that I hesitate a little and start to choose my words with extra care.

'You know that I owe such a lot to my old teacher, Mr Potter? He had faith in me as a youngster. He's the one who really taught me how to be a writer. It's no exaggeration to say that I am where I am today because of him. So, when Mrs Potter told me about her concerns for her daughter… well, I felt I just had to help…'

I'm watching Monica closely, trying to judge her reaction and break the news to her gently. She likes our lifestyle. She enjoys the finer things of life. And I know she's not going to be happy about us giving away so much of our money. I'm certain of all that. Certain. But I'm wrong.

'And you said you'd provide the money for her care, didn't you?'

Her interruption takes me by surprise and I prepare myself for her displeasure at my decision. When Monica is unhappy about something she doesn't hold back. I nod apologetically and acknowledge that that's exactly what I did. But she's far from being annoyed.

'O, Zander, I'm so proud of you.' She throws her arms round my neck and I can feel the tears trickling down her cheek and making my shirt damp. 'That was the right thing to do. And we can well afford to do it.'

We hold each other tightly for what seems a long time. And then we talk. We talk well into the small hours of the morning. We talk about our lifestyle: the money we spend on things we don't need; the clothes we buy and wear only a couple of times before we discard them; the food that fills our fridge and then gets thrown away when we realise that it's gone past its sell-by date. We talk about our marriage: our emotional immaturity as individuals and as a couple; our growing awareness that intimacy needs to involve so much more than what happens in the bedroom. And we talk about the satisfaction that even this one act of proposed generosity is giving us. As we talk and listen to each other in a way we've never done before, I catch a glimpse for the first time of the true worth of this woman whose emotional growth has been stunted by a damaging childhood but who has the potential to become so much more than merely the object of my sexual desire and the answer to my need for a mate. It's the start of a long journey together. It takes up the next few years of our lives and there are a few stumbles and wrong turns along the way. But it's an odyssey that brings us closer together as it leads us in a new direction.

Mrs Potter died two days after my visit. Her sister died less than a year later, but by that time we'd already set up a trust fund for Amy and settled her in an excellent care facility near to us in north London so that we could visit her regularly. But that's only the first step in our journey, and it's Monica who feels the call of the road ahead even more strongly than I do.

At first, I'm worried about this abrupt change in her and wonder if it will be short-lived. I know my grandfather, old Alec Binnie, believed in instant conversions, but I'm far from being convinced about such sudden turnarounds in people. My wife, however, shows no signs of backsliding from her new-found commitment to altruism. On the contrary, she grows ever more resolute in her zeal to do good to others. Within months, she takes the initiative in deciding that we should donate a tenth of our income to organisations working with the severely disabled. Not satisfied with that, she employs her skills of persuasion, which have previously been directed exclusively to bending my will to do her bidding, in convincing people she knows in the fashion industry to work with her in arranging a series of events to raise funds for a variety of charities working in that field. By the summer of 2007, in memory of Byron Abercrombie-Brydges, the best friend I ever had, and with the approval and support of his parents, we've established Byron's Buddies, a charitable foundation that provides resources and funds to organisations and charities working to combat the scourge of AIDS in the UK and overseas.

To the surprise of everyone who's ever known her, including me, the petulant, self-centred, childlike woman, whose sole concern has been to look as beautiful as possible in public, blossoms into Monica Lonan-Bennings, the charismatic and creative CEO of a charity that's beginning to make an impact out of proportion to its size and to engage the participation of some of the most influential players in the fashion industry. And all the while, as her public profile as the face of Byron's Buddies is increasing, my literary career is soaring to undreamed-of levels. Liberated from the niggling doubts about the origins of my first novel, I'm writing with a freedom and fluency that I've never experienced before. There are moves afoot for the film adaptation of my first book and my latest novel has just been published to general critical acclaim. At last I can close the door on the past and walk confidently in the present. And who knows what the future might bring?

chapter 16
secrets and lies
2013

We're sitting on the patio, under the shade of the cherry trees in the garden of our Hampstead cottage. It's a warm and sunny spring day in early April and, lubricated by a bottle of fine red wine, the interview is going well. *The Clarion* is a quality Sunday broadsheet and Damian Martyn is a highly respected journalist whose relaxed and amiable manner belies his hard-earned and well-deserved reputation for getting his subjects to talk freely and reveal truths about themselves that they've never shared with the public previously and that they sometimes later regret. But there's been nothing in our conversation so far to concern me. A positive article appearing under his name will do my standing with the wider public no harm at all. He's interested in who I am as a person, what it is within me that craves the release of writing, and what, now that I have enough money to be comfortable, motivates me to sit alone in front of my laptop churning out the words day after day.

The interview ranges from my time working as an undertaker to what Damian describes as my 'unusually prolific output' and how the last seven years have been particularly productive. I tell him about my 'B of the Bang' moment at the beginning of 2005 that provided the momentum for all that I've done since then in terms of both my literary output and my charitable work. But it's when I relate the story of the first time I made any money from my writing as a fifteen-year-old and the impact that the object of my schoolboy satire, Mr Potter, subsequently had on my life and future career, that he seems particularly interested. That's just the kind of anecdote, he tells me, that he's always looking for. Something that shows the human face of an interviewee and gives an insight into what set them on their path in life.

I must have been answering his questions for well over an hour when he switches off his voice recorder and proposes that we take a break. Since this interview is to be the main feature in their magazine section next Sunday, his editor is keen to get some shots that will add visual interest to the article. Damian suggests that we get those done now and allow Greg, the photographer, to leave for his next assignment before we round things off with a few additional questions. I'm never sure exactly what the reading public expect an author to look like, but I pull on a dark-blue sweater over my T-shirt and jeans and hope I've got the right look – casual enough to be relaxed and at ease, but sufficiently thoughtful to fit what I assume to be the popular image of a serious writer.

Greg, to my relief, isn't one of those photographers who takes hours to set up a shot. He works quickly, gathers his gear together and shakes my hand before heading quickly to his car. I turn my attention back to my interviewer, expecting a couple of general questions just to clarify anything that's not been clear before we wrap up the interview.

'We won't be needing this any more.' Damian smiles and holds up his voice recorder to show it to me before dropping it into his bag. 'It's a good *aide memoire*, especially when I can't decipher my notes. But sometimes it gets in the way when you really want to talk at greater depths.'

The phrase 'at greater depths' makes me a little uncomfortable. Why is he so anxious to put me at my ease when the interview is at an end?

'I thought we were pretty much done. Thought you'd got everything you needed for the article.'

'Oh, I do. That's all fine. I'll give you a call in a couple of days when I've got it ready and let you see the draft. Make sure there's nothing that makes you unhappy.' The smile has gone from his face and he's wearing a more serious expression than I'd expect from a journalist doing a feature for a Sunday magazine piece. 'No, it's not directly about the interview. But there is something I want to talk to you about. Off the record, if you like. That's why I thought it best to get rid of Greg before we chat.'

My first instinct is to tell him that I don't do 'off the record' interviews. But there's something about his demeanour that makes me hesitate. I can't quite put my finger on what it is. He's certainly not aggressive or threatening, but I can see he's not going to be put off. I decide that it's wise to hear what he has to say, even if I need to be on my guard. Maybe there's something he wants to warn me about. A problem with Byron's Buddies perhaps. We've been going long enough to know that you can't be too careful about making sure that everything you do as a charity stays well within the spirit as well as the letter of the law. So I sit down again, anxious to convey the impression that I'm totally unconcerned about whatever it is he's going to say to me.

'Well, fire away. Though I can't think what it is you want to talk about.'

He pauses before he speaks, and I can sense that he's watching me carefully, ready to scrutinise my reaction to his words when they come.

'A colleague of mine at *The Clarion* used to work for a little publishing company called Bex Press that went belly-up last year. It was one of his first jobs after he graduated and before he got into journalism. They had premises in a back street somewhere just off the Edgware Road. Mostly published stuff for first-time authors. Never had any bestsellers or anything like that. But they were quite good at putting out stuff that catered to different niche markets. And that kept them afloat for a good thirty years, which has to be some kind of success. You know how cut-throat the publishing world can be.'

As I listen, I'm trying to work out what this has to do with me and why we need to be alone for him to tell me about it. The only thing I can think is that the demise of this publishing house has left some of their writers unpaid and struggling financially. Maybe he's about to ask if I'm willing, as a well-known author, to front some charity event he's got in mind. But that still doesn't sound like something that demands this level of confidentiality. He smiles reassuringly and I know he can see from my face how puzzled I am as to where this is going.

'Anyhow, to get to the point, my colleague – the one who worked for this publishing company for a few years in his younger days – knew from his time there that they'd missed out on some big opportunities to strike oil. Historical material, political commentary, popular science, biography – they were quite good at picking up writers in those genres that the big firms weren't willing to take on. But they made some real gaffes when it came to fiction. He remembered at least two manuscripts that they rejected out of hand that later got picked up by other publishers and went on to sell really well. If they'd been better at spotting that kind of thing, they might still be in business.'

By this time, I'm more confused than ever as to how any of this is relevant to me. I'm also growing increasingly uncomfortable. I've no idea where this is heading, but I'm absolutely sure that Damian Martyn knows exactly where he's going with it. He's playing me like some experienced angler whose got plenty of time, allowing his line to run out until the right moment when the unsuspecting fish takes the bait and he can reel it in. The problem with that metaphor, I see immediately, is that I don't have the option of swimming off in the opposite direction. Other than closing the conversation abruptly and asking him to leave, which I sense wouldn't be the wisest course of action, I've no means of escape.

'So this affects me how?' I ask, shrugging my shoulders and hoping that I sound unconcerned even though I can feel my heart beginning to beat a little faster.

'Well, here's the reason I wanted to talk to *you* about this…' He gives a little cough as if to clear his throat. But I know he's delaying, deliberately increasing the pressure on me, making me wait. 'My colleague also remembered that they rarely if ever returned any of the manuscripts that they received. Often didn't even send a rejection note. Just filed them away in a cupboard and forgot about them. Now, he guessed there might well be stuff still locked away there and forgotten. Stuff that could be of interest. He wondered if there might be a story in it. You know… a neglected masterpiece waiting to see the light of day…'

The way he leaves the words hanging at the end of that last sentence makes the tension I'm feeling almost unbearable. Which I'm sure is exactly what he wants. It's a warm day, but I know it's not the temperature that's causing me to perspire. He's dragging this out and he's waiting for me to crack. I do my best to look unconcerned.

'So, my colleague manages to persuade them to give him access to the archives before they vacate the premises. His old employer who's now in his eighties is just glad that someone's willing to get rid of the stuff for him. And this is where it starts to get really interesting…'

He's doing it again. Letting the words dangle like the hook on the end of the line.

He's getting ready to reel me in – *slowly*.

'Most of what he finds is of little or no value in literary terms. Stuff from people with little talent, most of whom are long dead. Heaps of pages fit only for the shredder. But there's a couple of manuscripts that really grab his attention. One in particular. One that had been submitted by a William C Potter who, I'm guessing, is one and the same as your old schoolteacher.' His expression hardens and he fixes his eyes on me. 'Well, to be honest with you, Mr Bennings, I'm not guessing. My colleague has checked the correspondence that went with the manuscript and there's no room for any doubt.'

I want to say something – anything – that will halt the momentum of this one-sided conversation and what I fear will be its inevitable conclusion. But my brain can't put the words in order and my mouth is too dry to speak, even if I could think of what to say. Damian pauses for just a moment and then continues.

'That manuscript bears a remarkable resemblance to your first successful novel, *Bald Man on a Squeaky Bike*. The plot's the same, apart from a few minor alterations that don't change anything significantly. There are whole paragraphs that are almost identical. Sentences and phrases that match.'

Now it's time to land his catch. However much I squirm and try to wriggle free, he knows he's got me.

'Now, even if I put the best gloss on all this, even recognising the influence of this man who you tell me was your mentor, even acknowledging that you might well subconsciously have imbibed much of his style… none of that is enough to explain the incredibly close similarity between your bestselling novel and his rejected manuscript. Mr Bennings, it's time for you to be honest about what happened here. Unless you have an explanation – and I can't think of one that would satisfy me, or anyone else for that matter – you're open to the accusation of shameless plagiarism. My colleague hasn't spoken to anyone else about this, other than me. But don't be under any illusions here. This is too big a story to be filed away somewhere. I *will* write it and I've no doubt my editor will publish it when I put it on his desk. But I'm giving you a chance to talk to me before that happens.'

I feel physically sick. For a moment or two I think I might actually throw up in front of Damian Martyn. I close my eyes and put my hand over my mouth until the wave of nausea subsides. I have sufficient clarity of mind to ask just one question. There might still be a way to get off the hook.

'You keep referring to your "colleague" who'd worked in the publishing business in the past. But there isn't really a "colleague", is there? It was you who found the manuscript, wasn't it?'

He smiles and nods, explaining that he was just employing a little bit of what he calls 'journalistic licence'. A technique he sometimes uses to let the interviewee know that there's no personal agenda in his questioning. He's simply engaging in the necessary task of investigative journalism. His response isn't sympathetic, but neither is it antagonistic. Trying to deny his accusation would be pointless, but there might be room for some negotiation.

'Damian, this isn't quite how you're making it look.' I'm trying to sound calm, but I can hear my voice wavering as I speak. 'I was young. I was under pressure to produce something. I'd gone through a series of rejections. And, as you've said, Mr Potter was my mentor. There was a special bond between us. And I really felt that in some way what I did was honouring his memory and all he'd done for me. That may not make sense to you. It doesn't make complete sense to me now either. With the benefit of hindsight, I can see that I wasn't thinking rationally at the time. It was a wrong thing to do. But I was a young man under pressure. Surely you can understand that.'

He takes his time before answering. And I watch him closely, looking for anything that might signal that he's

211

wavering in his determination to break the story. But, as he begins to speak again, neither his expression nor his words offer me any comfort.

'OK. I hear what you're saying. But even if I take what you've just said at face value – and I'm certainly not saying that I do – I can't ignore the fact that you've had years to reflect on what you did. Years to acknowledge the truth. Years to come clean with the public, with the people who've spent good money on what they believed was a book written by you. The bottom line is that you've become a wealthy man on the back of this deception. The success of all your books that have followed have been built on the reputation you gained with that first one. And I'm not the only person to think that *Bald Man on a Squeaky Bike* is better than any of your later work.'

'But there's a question you need to ask yourself,' I counter, ignoring his last remark. 'What will be achieved if you publish this? It'll cause harm to a lot of people. It's not just that it'll damage my reputation or take away the pleasure that a lot of readers find in my books. Think about my wife and how it will hurt her. Think about Byron's Buddies and all the good causes we support. All that will be harmed or even ruined completely if you break this story.'

He looks at me, stony-faced, and shakes his head slowly. My appeal has fallen on deaf ears, and I'm left searching for anything that might persuade him to change his mind. I dismiss the analogy of a fish hooked on the angler's line. That picture leaves no hope of escape. From somewhere deep in my subconscious, I conjure up the comic book image of the youthful trespasser intent on stealing apples from the orchard who's cornered by a ferocious guard dog, it's tongue lolling from the side of its mouth, its teeth bared and ready to sink into the seat of the intruder's trousers. His plight is desperate and his fate, it seems, is sealed. Nothing can change the nature of the savage beast standing in front of him. But it can be distracted by something it finds much more attractive and satisfying than biting the flesh of a mere boy. The comic strip artist comes to the rescue. A slab of raw meat appears in the hand of the frightened lad. He throws it to the dog who pounces on this unexpected treat and lets the intruder make his escape. I'm in a very tight corner, but maybe I can throw out the kind of raw meat that will distract a journalist hungry for a scoop. I know it's a risk, but I'm getting desperate.

'Look, Damian, you're a man of the world. You know what life's all about. We all want to make a decent living. We all cut corners at times. I can make it worth your while to bury this. Let's agree a price. You can walk away with far more money than you'd ever earn from publishing this story.'

His unyielding expression changes to a look of pity. For a split second I think I've broken free, that he'll take up my offer, and that this is what he's been hoping for all along. It's not an exclusive exposé he wants after all. He's got his eye on the main chance. He's looking to make some money out of his lucky find at Bex Press. But what I interpret as sympathy quickly morphs into an expression of utter disdain. He shakes his head as if in disbelief at my words. And when he speaks, there is no mistaking the bitter contempt in his voice.

'Mr Bennings, I've shown you a great deal of respect by coming to you before I break this story. I've just given you the opportunity to explain your actions, to come clean, to cooperate with me and use my article as a chance to confess what you've done and apologise to the public. And you respond by insulting me with an attempt to bribe me. I'm a journalist. It's my job to shine a light into dark places, to expose corruption, to seek out the truth. And no amount of money will distract me from that. I don't know the full extent of your wealth, but I can tell you this: if you were ten times richer than you are, you still wouldn't have enough money to buy me.'

He gets up, takes hold of his bag, and begins to walk away. There has to be some way I can get him to change his mind. I take hold of his arm and plead with him not to go, assuring him that we can sort this out. But he refuses to listen. There's nothing more to talk about, he insists, pushing me aside and hurrying across the lawn. It'll take him no more than a minute to walk down the path that wraps around the cottage. The panic is rising within me, taking me over completely, stifling every other thought and emotion. All that matters is that I stop him before he reaches the gate and gets into his car. I run after him and catch up with him in the narrow passage that runs between the side of the house and the tall hedge that separates us from the adjoining property. It's the perfect place to block his progress. I position myself between him and the gate and refuse to let him go any further. I'm only vaguely aware of how loudly I'm shouting and swearing and my rational mind is trying to warn me that we can be overheard by our neighbours whose house is less than sixty feet away on the other side of the hedge. But the voice of reason is drowned out by the surging waves of anxiety that are flooding over me.

'You've got to calm down.' Damian Martyn is speaking quietly and he repeats the sentence two or three times. 'You're only going to make things worse for yourself.'

His words don't make any sense to me because I can't imagine how things could be any worse than they are at this moment. I spread my arms out, determined not to let him pass, but he keeps moving forward until I can feel his body leaning into mine, trying to push me out of the way. That's when I snap completely and abandon myself to the blind panic and all-consuming rage that have me in their grip. I don't know exactly what happens after that. There's a struggle as he tries to get past me and we wrestle each other to the ground. I can smell his sweat as we roll back and forth, locked in a violent embrace from which neither of us can free ourselves. The gravel from the path is tearing the skin from my arms and his fingernails are digging into my face. One of my teeth is loose and there's the metallic taste of blood in my mouth. Somehow, he wriggles free and gets to his feet. I must not let him escape. Before he can break into a run, I lunge at him and grab him round the ankles, pulling him back to the ground. That's all I mean to do, just to stop him from getting away. But he's been leaning forward, trying to run. That's what causes him to lurch to the left with such force. I can neither describe nor forget that sound – the noise of his skull smashing into the wall of the cottage. The sight of his blood slowly trickling down the brickwork in bright red rivulets will haunt my dreams for as long as I live.

In an instant the anger drains from my body, leaving only a hollow feeling of utter exhaustion. From somewhere I summon up the energy to crawl on my hands and knees and bend over his body. The gravel is stained with the blood that continues to seep from the wound on his head. I try to feel his pulse and listen for his breathing, but his body is very still and his face is very pale. The reality of the situation begins to dawn on me and for a minute I've no idea what I should do. My first thought is that I need to make everything look normal before Monica comes home. Clear away all the mess. Get Damian off the path and into his car. Hose the blood from the wall and rake over the gravel. Make it look like nothing has happened. But I don't do any of that. I stand up, stumble into the cottage, pick up the phone and dial 999. And when the operator asks me which emergency service I require, I ask for an ambulance and explain that a guest in my home has had a fall and may be seriously injured. Then I go back outside, kneel down beside his body, and pray that Damian Martyn will live.

chapter 17
history lessons
2013

It's July and, after several weeks of changeable weather, we're in the middle of a heatwave. There's a headline in the newspaper in front of me announcing that the temperature is higher in London today than in half a dozen places in the world to which British holidaymakers have flown in pursuit of sun, sea and sand. I'm glad to be where I am and, like the weather, my mood has begun to improve. I'm certainly not dancing and singing in the sunshine, but the dark thoughts that have hung over me for the last couple of months have lifted enough for me to begin to face my present situation, even if I cannot contemplate the future.

This is the first time I've felt able to venture back into the garden since that fateful afternoon back in April. And it isn't just the sight of the mercury rising in the barometer that's lifted my spirits. There is good news – better news than I could have imagined a few weeks ago – from the hospital. At the beginning of the month, Damian Martyn emerged from a medically induced coma, and the word I'm hearing is that his speech is returning and he's able to converse with the medical staff and his close family. Of course, it'll be a long road back to full health, but his doctors are saying that there's reason to hope that he will recover sufficiently to resume his life without significant or permanent brain damage.

The police, of course, have been here on a number of occasions. They've examined and photographed the scene of the accident carefully and interviewed me at length several times. I've tried to be as honest as I can, even though the gaps in my memory make it impossible for me to give them an accurate account of exactly what happened that day. In the course of their questioning, I've had to tell them about the conversation that took place between Damian and myself at the end of the interview and how it led to a scuffle between us that culminated in the unfortunate accident. And, rather than wait for the story to leak as it inevitably would have done, I've issued a statement through my lawyer admitting my deception over my first novel and apologising to my readers. How this will affect future sales of my books and whether my reputation will ever recover, I've no idea.

At the moment, however, that's the least of my concerns. After trying unsuccessfully for so long to start a family, Monica and I are expecting our first child, and I'm desperately worried as to what effect all this will have on her and on her pregnancy. As she's done so often over these last nine years, she continues to surprise me. I noted when I was reflecting on the three generations who've gone before me that it's been the women in my family who've often held things together, who've remained strong when everything around them seemed to be falling apart, who've kept walking steadily forward when their menfolk have stumbled and fallen. Little did I realise how true this would turn out to be in my own life. The childlike bride who had no more lofty ambition than to walk up the aisle to a fanfare at her fairy-tale wedding has become the mature woman who manages to combine being a faithful wife with the demands of heading up a fair-sized charity. In recent years, she's gradually cut back on her modelling work to allow herself time to concentrate on running Byron's Buddies. And now she's keeping me afloat when, left to myself, I fear I would have drowned in a sea of despair.

For the last three months I've found it impossible to make any progress on the book I'm supposed to be working on. None of the little tricks I've employed in the past when I've needed something to cure an attack of writer's block make any difference now. I sit at my desk trying to do what I've always loved doing – putting words together to tell a story. But nothing happens. My mind is as blank as the screen in front of me and my fingers sit idle and motionless on the keyboard. After an hour of this pointless pretence of writing, I turn off my laptop and walk away, more depressed than I was when I sat down. It's little wonder that I'm getting absolutely nowhere. What hope do I have of producing interesting and meaningful fiction when I can't handle the confusing reality of my life. Until I find a way of dealing with that, I don't see any hope of making progress.

That's why today, in near desperation, I've gone into the desk drawer and retrieved those three blue-covered exercise books that my grandfather, Alec Binnie, gave me when I spent the weekend with him and my grandmother in Bellmill all those years ago. I've glanced at them on numerous occasions over the years and thought to myself that I would return to them and give them my full attention when the time was right. *I know that time is now.* But I'm not reading them, as I had thought I would do, to find characters and incidents that I can make use of and fictionalise in a novel. No, I need them to help me make sense of my own life. At first the lethargy that's making it impossible for me to write with any enthusiasm makes it just as hard for me to read with any interest. But I persevere and gradually the simple linear narrative, painstakingly researched and meticulously recorded by a coalminer with little more than a basic education, begins to capture my attention. The people whose lives are told on these pages are *my* family. This is *their* story. And these events are what have made *my* story possible.

I allow my grandfather to lead me as I follow Sandy Binnie from his one-roomed home in a tenement building in Bellmill and the happy routine of life as a grocer's assistant in Tommy Maxwell's shop to the bloody Battle of the Somme where things are changed forever by the randomly destructive power of an enemy artillery shell launched into the air by a soldier on the other side of No Man's Land; a soldier who was himself nothing more than a pawn in this dehumanising conflict and who would have had no idea of what the result of his action would be on my great-grandfather. My tears flow for Sandy's sad decline and his untimely death at the age of forty-five, and my heart swells with pride when I reflect on the dogged faithfulness and sheer grit of the woman he married. Peggy Binnie is my great-grandmother and I am grateful that something of her must flow through my own veins and form some part of my own personality.

My grandfather's account of his own life is even more moving. As I read, I have to keep reminding myself that I have actually met this man who writes with such humility and in such deceptively powerful prose. I have met this man who never went to war but whose courage as he descends into the darkness of a Lanarkshire coalmine every day of his working life is no less deserving of my respect than that of his father who fought for king and country on the battlefields of France. I have met this man whose allegiance to the truths in which he believes stands out like a beacon in a working-class town where hard-working, hard-drinking men, with little time for religion, nonetheless hold him in high regard. I have met this man whose desire to be good is the ruling passion of his life. I have met this man who writes of his brother, Bobby, the militant Communist whose path took him in a different direction and with whom he often passionately disagreed, with a respect for his sibling's convictions and an acute awareness that seeking after God and the struggle for justice are two sides of the same coin. I have met this man who writes about Irene Moffat, the youthful songster who caught his eye and stole his heart and shared his life for more than sixty years, with an exquisite tenderness worthy of a love song. Yes, I have met Alec Binnie. And though his faith is something to which I am unlikely ever to attain, I long to live in my day a life that echoes the integrity of his.

But it's the last of those blue exercise books that I find the most affecting and disturbing of the three. It's like watching one of those old 35mm home movies from the 1960s or 1970s as a child. You realise, to your surprise, that the figure on the screen is indeed the middle-aged adult sitting next to you on the sofa, but younger than you've ever seen them or even imagined them. The flickering image and the unnaturally bright colours give a dreamlike quality to what you're watching that is uncomfortably disorientating. It's as if some ancient sorcery is transporting you to a time before you were born and to a place where you have no right to be. My dad – the man who keeps his emotions in check and discloses little about himself – emerges out of the mists of the past as the rebellious teenager who turns his back on home and family. My grandfather's written recollections become for me a magical means of time-travel that allows me to see the respectable middle-aged undertaker as he was fifty years ago – a talented footballer with the world at his feet. I understand, as never before, what has made him the man he is. And yet, at the same time, I find the gulf between who he was and what he has become perplexing. He is a much more complex figure than I thought he was and my relationship with him has become correspondingly more nuanced and more difficult to define.

And throughout this family history, across a century and three generations, there are truths that begin to surface that are unchanged by the passing of time. We live in a world that is, at best, uncertain and, at worst, dangerous, perhaps even malignant. That treacherous unpredictability might manifest itself in the blast of an enemy shell on the battlefield, the careless two-footed tackle of an overeager opponent on the football field, or in a thousand and one other ways. But it is an ever-present reality that means the hopes and dreams of any one of us can be destroyed in a moment. There is more than enough in my family's story to show that there is beauty and love and faithfulness and kindness in this world. But there is also ample evidence that this is not a paradisal garden. Nor is this fragile planet a place in which it is always easy, even for people of faith, to see the hand of a benevolent deity. Sandy Binnie was not the first, nor will he be the last, to jettison his cargo of neat and tidy answers in the face of the storms that blow up out of nowhere and threaten our very existence.

But there is a truth even more disturbing than this, a truth that is borne out, not just by the story of my family, but by the history of the human race. It isn't only the world around us that can be dangerous and destructive. There is something within us – even the best of us – that threatens our happiness and can devastate our relationships with others. The war that Sandy Binnie was caught up in didn't happen by chance or because of some cruel misalignment of the planets. The spark that set Europe aflame in 1914 came from the gun of an angry young man, the gun that was aimed, with fatal consequences, at the heir to the Austro-Hungarian Empire. If his mother had had her way, the assassin would have been called Spiro in memory of her deceased brother. But she yielded to the pleas of her parish priest who persuaded her that the sickly child in her arms would have the chance of a better life if he was named after the archangel Gabriel. Alas, even bearing the name of the greatest of the angelic beings could not restrain the dark urges that incited Gavrilo Princip to fire the shot that would set in motion the chain reaction of death and destruction that cost the lives of millions.

Alec and Bobby Binnie had different priorities that took them in opposite directions. But each of them was responding to the twin realities that confront all of us. Alec recognised in his own heart the destructive power of the self-centred bias in every one of us: his faith taught him to identify that malignant force as sin that needs to be forgiven and overcome. And Bobby saw all around him the injustice of poverty and oppression: his political philosophy told him that this dislocation of society needed nothing less than a revolution in the world order. Sages and philosophers, politicians and theologians, moralists and ordinary people trying to make the best of life will continue to debate how to deal with them. But what is beyond disagreement is this: when those two forces coincide – the destructive urges within us and the dangerous world around us – the results can be no less catastrophic than the collision of the great tectonic plates beneath the surface of our planet that cause the earth to break and erupt beneath our feet.

At such times, the best of us can be reduced to a living parody of who and what we really want to be. Caught up in the horrors of what is euphemistically called 'The Great War' (whoever thought of describing something so horrendous as 'great'?), a deeply religious man like Sandy Binnie lost his faith and became a sad and embittered caricature of himself. Faced with his son's ambition to be a professional footballer, a good man like my grandfather failed to handle the family tensions with the understanding and compassion that would have prevented the breakdown in family life that lasted so many years. Confronted first with the resistance of his parents and then by the injury that curtailed his progress as a footballer, my father's impetuosity and pride robbed him of the joy of his youth.

And what of me, Zander Bennings? I have a different name, I live in a different time, I move in different social circles, and I enjoy a standard of living that surpasses even that of my parents and would amaze my grandfather and great-grandfather. But my part in this story reveals all too clearly that despite all the changes, despite everything that we would view as progress, I live in the same broken world and share the same flawed human nature as my forebears. I take some comfort in my belief that the charity we have set up and in which Monica and I have invested so much of our time and money is playing a part in healing this broken world, making it a little less dangerous and a safer place for people to live in. But what's happened in these recent months has brought me to the place where I'm forced to acknowledge that it's also been a way of compensating for my failure to address the truth about myself and what I've done. If I'm really honest, I have to accept that it's been even more of an evasion than a compensation. I've used Byron's Buddies and the other good things we've done, worthy as they've been in themselves, as a way of justifying the deception I've been carrying out on the public for all these years. I've been persuading myself that good has resulted from what I did the night I decided to pass off Mr Potter's story as my own. I've pushed it out of my mind and told myself that everything's alright.

But when I saw Damian Martyn lying unconscious by the wall of my cottage, the blood oozing from the wound in his head, the full extent of my culpability dawned on me. My blind rage at his intention to tell the world of my deceit, my ruthless determination to stop him at any cost, my callous willingness to pile one act of wrongdoing on another to protect the lie I had maintained for so long shocked me to the core of my being. I saw myself as never before and I did not like what I saw. If that is my own reaction to my character and my conduct, I can only imagine what the verdict of others will be. I know that the police will interview Damian as soon as his doctors say he's well enough to face their questioning. Depending on his recollection of events, I fear that I will be facing serious consequences. The prospect fills me with dread.

chapter 18
fallen icons
2014

I cannot imagine any human activity that's more detached from normal life and everyday reality than a trial in an English Crown Court. Every aspect of its formalised proceedings, every interaction between the bewigged actors in its elaborate rituals, every phrase spoken in the legal jargonese that's barely comprehensible to ordinary mortals – all presumably intended to create a sense of awe and respect for the due processes of law – can make those caught up in its apparently other-worldly transactions feel powerless in the face of forces over which they have no control and at the mercy of experts who have no real interest in them as individuals.

The splendid robes and the elevated position of the judge at the front of the court endue him with a god-like status in this alternative universe-within-a-room. And though he instructs the 'twelve good men and true' who make up the jury that they, and they alone, must weigh up the evidence and decide on the guilt or innocence of the accused, it's difficult to avoid the conclusion that, like God Himself, he will have the final and decisive word. The prosecution and defence barristers confront each other in verbal combat, their weapons of choice being their well-rehearsed eloquence, their quick-witted repartee, and their impressive ability to quote from the more obscure points of the law. But this contest will not result in injury or loss to either of the combatants. Like the re-enactments of medieval jousting that draw crowds to theme parks up and down the country on summer days, this is a performance that's designed, if not to entertain, then certainly to impress an audience – in this case, the jurors. And while all this is going on, the people who should be the main actors in the drama – the accused, the victim, the witnesses – sit helplessly on the margins, with little influence on the proceedings and even less idea of what's going on.

If I were sitting in the public gallery, I would be observing this spectacle with interest. Like many a storyteller before me, I would recognise immediately that there's a ready supply of material here that would add drama to a compelling tale. But I'm not an observer in the public gallery. I'm the defendant in the dock, facing a charge of Grievous Bodily Harm, an offence that carries a maximum penalty of sixteen years in prison. It's eleven o'clock on the morning of Monday 31st March and we're waiting for the jury to return their verdict, having completed their deliberations. It's taken them just under two hours to reach their verdict and I guess this means that one way or the other, there's been little disagreement among them.

My barrister has tried to encourage me by telling me that so far 'everything's worked out well for us' and that there's good reason to be optimistic. We've been fortunate in regard to the speed with which the matter has come to court. The doctors didn't consider that Damian Martyn was well enough to be interviewed by the police until November and consequently I wasn't formally charged until the middle of December. Three months, apparently, is not long to wait for the wheels of the legal system to grind. And the trial itself has been mercifully brief, having lasted just over a week. There were, of course, no eyewitnesses to the alleged offence, other than my neighbour who heard the shouting but saw nothing. So, apart from the input of police officers and a number of experts, those who've been called to the witness stand have been able to provide only character references or other background information that's considered relevant to my credibility.

My parents have been present throughout the trial. I can only guess what this must be costing them emotionally but I've been grateful for their support. Monica came on the first day, determined to show her support for me, but our baby is due in just over a week and, to my relief, her doctor has persuaded her that coming to court each day would not be wise at this advanced stage of her pregnancy. Inevitably there's a great deal of media interest in the proceedings and I can only guess what the headlines will be if the verdict goes against me. The trial itself has centred on the issue of what exactly happened in that narrow passageway running alongside the cottage. My barrister, working from my honest recollection of the events, has put forward the defence that Damian Martyn struck the first blow as he tried to push me out of the way and get past me, and that there was no intention on my part to cause him any injury.

My sole objective was to persuade him not to leave until we could resolve the issue between us. The fact that his head struck the wall in the scuffle between us was entirely accidental, a result of my attempts at self-defence.

The prosecution, however, have argued strongly that I was determined to do anything to stop Damian leaving that afternoon to prevent him from revealing the cover-up in which I was engaged, that I was the aggressor, and that the manner in which I attacked him was designed to cause him serious injury. Both sides have summoned expert witnesses to give their different opinions on the nature of the damage to his skull, on the angle of impact and the velocity with which that impact took place. My best guess is that those supporting the prosecution case will carry more weight. And I suspect that there are two factors that will sway the jury more than anything else. There is the undeniable truth that I was seeking to maintain a deception I had been perpetrating on the public for years. And there is the sight of Damian in the witness box, his ponderous speech and laboured movements making the ongoing effects of his injury painfully obvious.

But the waiting is almost over. My heart begins to beat faster as the jury file back into the courtroom and take their places on my right-hand side. I want to stare straight ahead, but I can't help glancing quickly at my parents and I notice that they're holding hands. Somehow that sight threatens to demolish the emotional wall I'm trying to erect around me and I look away quickly. I stand as instructed and hear the question from the clerk of the court to the foreman of the jury.

'Have you reached a verdict on which you all agree?'

The affirmative response is immediate, and it elicits the question to which everything that's happened in the preceding week has been relentlessly leading.

'Do you find the defendant guilty or not guilty?'

The words hang in the air as the foreman of the jury hesitates for a second before delivering his answer. It's a moment like nothing I've ever experienced before or since, a moment in which everything around me seems to stand still, a moment that will change my life forever, a moment that ends with the word I've been half-expecting but dreading.

'Guilty.'

After that I feel suddenly and oddly detached from it all. The tension that's been gripping me has gone. The wave of emotion that I've been anticipating and against which I've been bracing myself never comes. Some kind of psychological defence mechanism has kicked into action. In my mind I'm no longer the defendant. I've become a detached onlooker, watching the prisoner in the dock and observing what's happening around him. The members of the jury, relieved that their responsibilities are at an end, are being thanked for their deliberations and dismissed. My mother is quietly weeping into a handkerchief and my father is putting his arm around her to comfort her. Damian Martyn's face has an expression that I can't interpret clearly. An expression that's somewhere between relief and regret. The judge is saying that he will adjourn until the morning, to allow himself time overnight to consider the circumstances surrounding the case, before delivering his sentence. I stumble down the steps from the dock and into the cell below wondering what all this has to do with me.

It isn't until after I've been locked up and left alone with my thoughts that the reality of my situation breaks in on me. I'm a convicted criminal lying awake in a desolate emotional void, the long night hours between a guilty verdict and the sentence that will be pronounced in a few hours' time. These are the most unsettling and uncertain hours I've ever experienced. The life that I've lived for the past twenty years is over. The future I've anticipated, even taken for granted, will never arrive. The reputation I've built over two decades lies in ruins. The good works that Byron's Buddies has been doing may come to a juddering halt. The child to whom my wife is about to give birth will learn as he grows older that his father was in prison when he was born. I am ashamed and afraid.

But, at the darkest hour, around two o'clock in the morning, when everything I've worked for and achieved seems lost, something begins to shift. And it takes me completely by surprise. My situation is exactly as I've just described it to myself. Nothing has altered *around* me. No one is unlocking the door and telling me that things have suddenly changed for the better, that this has all been a ghastly nightmare, that I'm free to go. Something, however, is changing *within* me. It takes me some time to work out what it is. But as the first light of dawn shines through the window, I recognise what is happening to me. And what I'm experiencing is a profound sense of relief. I know I am guilty. The jury has said so. The newspapers will announce it in banner headlines. My neighbours will gossip about it when they meet. My wife and parents will weep over it. I will carry my guilt with me into the courtroom in just a few hours. And the judge will sentence me to what he considers is the appropriate punishment for my guilt.

So why this sense of relief? Because at last I can drop the pretence I've been dragging with me, the self-deceit that's weighed on me like a heavy chain around my body. I don't know which of us – Damian Martyn or me – was recalling the sequence of events accurately and telling the jury honestly exactly what happened as he tried to leave my house. But it doesn't really make any difference. All I know for certain is that I was determined to stop him from leaving, determined to prevent him from publishing his article, determined to keep a tight lid on my deception. The truth is that I was guilty long before I laid a hand on Damian. It's not only that my conduct was morally reprehensible, that I'd dishonoured the man who was my mentor, that I was profiting from another man's work, that I was cheating my readers. It was all of those things. But it was so much more than that. It had become a *thing* in itself. A thing that had slowly but surely tightened its hold on me until it had me firmly in its grasp, controlling my thoughts and actions.

I owe a debt to Damian Martyn for breaking in on my life as he did with his threat to expose me. I owe a debt to the police officers who investigated my actions and brought charges against me. I owe a debt to the jurors who listened to the evidence and convicted me. I owe them all a debt because I can stop pretending, I can stop rationalising and I can face the reality of my guilt. Yes, I'm in prison. But I've been released from all that. I know, of course, that it doesn't mean that everything's now alright. I don't know what lies ahead of me and what a hard road I will have to walk. But it is a relief, nonetheless. It's like when you've been feeling really ill and you've been trying to persuade yourself that it's all in your imagination and that there's really nothing to worry about. But whatever it is, it won't go away. Eventually you go to see a doctor who tells you that it's serious – some terrible life-threatening disease – and that it could be terminal. He gives you no glib comforting clichés. He offers you no guarantee of an easy or instantaneous cure. But his sober judgement and his solemn words bring relief because he's named the *thing*. And if he can name it, he must know something about it. And, if he knows something about it, then maybe – just maybe – it can be dealt with. Maybe it can be cured. Or, if there's no cure, maybe there's a way of living with it. Or, if there's no way of living with it, then maybe there's a way of bearing it with dignity until the end comes. That's exactly what it feels like for me now that I've accepted my guilt.

Of course, I know that no one emerges from these experiences unchanged or unscathed. Wherever there's a cure, there's always a cost. Something has to be forfeited as the price for the freedom you've been given. There may be lingering after-effects of the treatment that saved your life. There may be things you did before, things you've done all your life, that you'll never be able to do again in quite the same way. You may have to reassess your values and your priorities and resign yourself to a new normality. It's no different as I break free from the deception that controlled my life and come to terms with the guilt that I have to acknowledge. And on this night, as I wait for the morning to bring my sentence, I know what that price will be for me. In fact, I've really known since the day almost two years ago when I ripped the cutting from the newspaper I was reading and slipped it into my wallet. As the daylight breaks into my cell, I take it out and read it again. It's an article about the fate of the *B of the Bang*, that curious bit of abstract public art I first saw on the television news bulletin back in January 2005. Alas, the iconic metal structure that inspired me to take my 'FIRST STEPS IN A NEW DIRECTION' has come to a sad and ignominious end. It's the kind of report that leaves you wondering whether you should laugh or cry.

> The *B of the Bang*, purchased by the city at a cost of almost £2 million, was originally branded 'a magnificent artistic statement' and was intended to symbolise a bold new start for Manchester. Today, however, we can reveal that it has finally reached an inglorious finale.
>
> Following a long and sorry chapter of accidents involving large pieces of metal falling to the ground with the risk of serious injury to unsuspecting passers-by, the *B of the Bang* is no more.
>
> The core and legs of the 184-foot structure were dismantled and placed in storage when it was taken down for safety reasons in February 2009. Now, three years later, councillors have admitted that they have been melted down for scrap metal, raising £17,000 for the city coffers. This will seem a poor return for taxpayers on their original £2 million investment.
>
> The 180 spikes that proved to be a nightmare to those responsible for health and safety and a danger to everyone who came close to the ill-fated sculpture are now locked away in what has

been described to this newspaper as 'a secret location'.
All in all, it's an ignominious ending to what at first seemed to Mancunians like a major addition to the city's unique collection of public art.

From the moment I took inspiration from *the B of the Bang*, resolving to work at my marriage, to get involved in charitable projects, to keep in close contact with my parents, to look for every opportunity to do good, it's been the symbol of the kind of man I've wanted to be, a towering visual expression of the values by which I've been trying to live. And now this overambitious sculpture lies in ruins, each broken piece providing indisputable evidence that those who designed and constructed it failed to foresee the flaws in their ill-conceived plans. And my overambitious and ill-conceived resolutions lie in ruins with it because, like them, I failed to see the flaw that would bring everything tumbling down around me. I imagined that my noble intentions and good deeds would be enough to compensate for the thing I was covering up. I was wrong. The harsh truth is that the flaw at the heart of my life has ultimately and inevitably brought everything tumbling down around my ears.

It's not the first time this has happened in my family. In my mind's eye, I can see my great-grandfather, Sandy Binnie, standing in a French field in 1915, shielding his eyes as he looked up at the statue of the Madonna and Child glinting in the morning sun and hanging precariously from the top of the cathedral in Albert. Like me, he too was facing the terrible truth that the things he thought he'd built his life upon were as fragile and broken as the shattered and fallen icon he was looking at.

chapter 19
doing time
2014–15

I don't know who first came up with the phrase 'doing time' as a euphemism for serving a prison sentence, but I'm pretty sure it didn't originate in the mind of some bearded sage or even in the imagination of someone like me who tries to use words to the best effect. It's such a perfect and succinct description of life behind bars that it must have come from the lips of someone who experienced the painfully slow passing of the minutes and hours in a place like this.

Oh, there are other things you have to do, of course. Washing, putting your clothes on in the morning, getting on with whatever tedious job you've been assigned by the officers, writing letters to your family, talking to other prisoners, exercising in the yard, lining up for what passes as food, sitting on the loo reading a magazine. And, of course, you're constantly guarding your words and actions carefully to make sure you don't upset any of the 'hard men', those violent criminals who are untamed by prison and who can make your life a misery and cause you serious injury if you upset them. In my case, one of the tasks to be done is trying to write, to keep a journal and hopefully make some use of this experience. But all of those things are at best distractions to take your mind off the one thing you're here to do, the real reason for locking you up. You're here to *do time*.

The politicians and lawmakers can debate what the purpose of prison life *should* be. Is it to punish the offender or to reform them? To make them pay their debt to society or to help them become a better person and a more productive citizen when they leave? But everyone who's ever been in a place like this knows what the truth is. It's about *doing time*. You've committed an offence and society understandably claims the right to take your most precious possession – your time. We don't hang people any longer in Britain. But what we do is to take a chunk of their lives – time they could be spending in meaningful work or pleasing leisure pursuits, time they will never get back again – and make them use that time in doing nothing but doing time itself.

It's getting towards the end of the custodial part of my sentence, just fifteen days to go until my release date on 1st October 2015, and I'm looking forward to returning to some kind of normal life where I can use my time purposefully again. Despite the boredom that's always lurking here and can sneak up on you at any moment, it's possible to survive without going completely stir-crazy. I've got through by following the rules, keeping as busy as I can and being as pleasant as possible to staff and prisoners. Anybody who's had any kind of fame in the outside world knows that in itself is enough to make you a marked man in here, and I quickly learned to keep a low profile and be just another prisoner. I've even managed to make one or two friends among the inmates, men who like reading and to whom I've been able to recommend some books they might enjoy, or give them some help in writing a difficult letter home.

The thing that's really kept me going has been the visits from Monica, who's stood by me throughout everything that's happened. As soon as I say that, I recognise that same motif that's run throughout this tale like an evocative counter-melody, contrasting and yet complementing the main theme of my story: while four generations of men have stumbled and sometimes fallen in the face of life's challenges, each one of them has been loved and supported by a woman who never gave up on them. And Monica has safely delivered the best gift I've ever received. Our son, Alexander William Bennings – his middle name is in honour of my old schoolteacher and mentor to whom I owe so much and whom I have so greatly wronged – is now a healthy, thriving toddler. We agreed that she would never bring him with her on her visits, as neither of us wants any image of this place, however hazy, to be imprinted on his memory. And I am more excited about seeing him and holding him for the first time than I've ever been about anything in my life to this point.

But right now, I have a visitor whom I'm glad to see. Although we've been infrequent attenders at his church (part of what he calls his 'auxiliary high-days-and-holidays congregation'), Alan Kibbell has come to see me every couple of months since I've been here. We settle ourselves at a table in the middle of the visiting hall and share the normal pleasantries before talking about my upcoming release. Alan reminds me of our conversation a decade ago sitting in front of Kenwood House when we talked about the opportunity to start again, do a U-turn and head in a different direction. And I respond by reflecting ruefully on how the resolutions I made back then seem to have helped to shape the path that's led me to this place. He thinks for a moment, then takes me aback by quoting a couple of lines from a poem that I know only too well, but that I never imagined would be part of any anthology of favourite verses for respectable clean-living Anglican vicars.

> Our life is a false nature – 'tis not in
> The harmony of things, – this hard decree,
> This uneradicable taint of sin …

He smiles at my surprise at his knowledge of this particular stanza.

'I don't know why you're so shocked, Zander. People like me are no different from people like you! We all suffer from the same weakness. My faith isn't about 'believing six impossible things before breakfast', as Lewis Carroll put it. Nor does it put a burden on me to require other people to reach a place of moral perfection. It starts from the point of recognising the truth about myself, the truth about all of us. We all mess things up at times, we all live with the terrible capacity to spoil our own lives and those of other people. That's "the hard decree", that's the "uneradicable taint of sin" that Byron was writing about. It's part of the human condition. One way or another, we'll have to struggle with it as long as we're alive.'

'Well, living where I'm living at the moment,' I reply with a bitter laugh, 'I can't argue with you on that one. At least we can wallow in despair together…'

'Oh no, it's quite the opposite,' he replies with a shake of his head. 'No, acknowledging that truth is the first step to finding hope. And acknowledging it for myself is what's driven me to what I believe is the truth. I'm not as funny as Lewis Carroll nor as poetically gifted as Byron, but I'm smart enough to have devised my own little formula for people who are looking for hope but who've been turned off by so much of what passes for religion. I use it on all my social media posts. In fact, I put it at the bottom of all my emails and any letters I send out these days. More often than not people want to know what it means, and that gives me the chance to speak about the thing I think people need to hear. I'll show you…'

He takes a pen out of his pocket and writes on the back of his left hand in bold letters: #ISoFaS. In response to my puzzled expression, he pushes up his sleeve, makes a simple drawing of a cross, and then slowly writes out his formula in full on his arm:

#Inexhaustible Source of Forgiveness and Strength

'Actually, that looks good,' he says, inspecting his arm approvingly. 'I've made up my mind that I'm going to have it properly tattooed on my arm. Just so I can make it part of who I am and carry the message with me wherever I go. And not just so other people see it whenever I roll my sleeve up, but as a constant reminder to myself of what my faith is all about.'

242

For a few moments, he holds his arm in a position where both of us can see it, before pushing his sleeve back down and putting his pen back in his pocket.

'You were talking about how your U-turn has gone all wrong and how you've ended up here. But, one way or another, that's the pattern for all of us. We want to do the right thing, so we set out in a new direction, and we mess things up all over again. And that can lead either to despair at our repeated failures or to a kind of moral treadmill where we end up exhausted by our efforts to do better. Worse still, in my book, some people, when they think that they've managed to do a little better, become proud of their own efforts and judgemental of the folk around them who are still struggling.'

The bell sounds for the end of visiting time and Alan gets up to leave. I try to tell him how grateful I've been to him for coming. But, without any warning, I become emotional and can't get the words out.

'You're welcome. I've enjoyed our conversations. And don't forget there will be a fee for my time.' He grins at me as one of the wardens reminds him that time's up and he needs to get a move on. 'We'll meet up for coffee or go for a pint together when you get home. You'll be paying, of course.'

I go back to the cell and record our conversation in my journal before I forget what we've talked about. I write down #ISoFaS, wondering how much truth, if any, is encapsulated in those seven characters. And I can't help but remember the preacher on that Sunday morning in Bellmill back in 1990 with his promise that not only can our wrong actions be forgiven, but that there is also power to overcome them. And I think to myself that, like Charlie

Parker in a New York jazz club, Alan Kibbell is riffing on an old tune that I've heard before.

chapter 20
home free
2015

It's another warm and sunny spring day in early April and I'm sitting on the patio, under the shade of the cherry trees in the garden of our Hampstead cottage. My wife is in the kitchen setting out the coffee cups and our two-year-old son is asleep in the nursery, having exhausted himself running up and down and rolling around on the lawn for most of the morning. The only things I can hear are the sounds of birdsong and the rustle of the leaves in the gentle breeze. It's an idyllic setting and it's difficult to imagine a more perfect place in which to chill out. But I'm tense and edgy at the thought of standing face to face with the visitor who'll be arriving in the next five minutes. When Harry Lipman called me about the request that had come to him, it had taken all his persuasive powers to get me to say yes. Protest as I might, he was adamant that I should agree to the meeting.

'Look, Zander my boy, it's not just that it might be useful for getting your career back on track, important as that is to both of us. But I honestly think it'll be good for you. Good for you as a person, I mean.' There was a pause and I could hear Harry on the other end of the phone stubbing out his cigar on the heavy glass ashtray that sits on his desk and needs to be emptied several times a day. I knew that if he was prepared to interrupt his normally nonstop cigar-smoking, he must be really keen for me to acquiesce. 'You know I'm pretty good at sussing these things out. He really wants to talk to you. I think he wants to put some kind of proposal to you. I'm sure he's not out to cause you any problems. My hunch is that you should say yes.'

In the end I agreed, as I usually end up doing to my agent's suggestions. There's no question that Harry's in the literary business to make money. He came up the hard way, a kid from a poor Jewish family living in the East End of London, with very little formal education, and he's got where he is by being willing to work and knowing how to cut a good deal for himself and his authors. But it's also undeniable that he's always loyal to his 'boys and girls'. He's certainly stuck by me over these recent years. Still addresses me as 'my boy' and still believes in me as a writer, despite his embarrassment when he had to admit to the world that I'd conned him with my first novel and that he'd been totally taken in by my deception.

I glance at my watch. It's just a couple of minutes off two o'clock, the time scheduled for the appointment. My nerves are getting the better of me, so I hurry into the cottage for a last-minute visit to the loo, and I realise that I should have gone earlier when I hear the doorbell ring as I'm drying my hands. I wait until I hear Monica show him into the lounge before I flush the loo, take a deep breath and walk out to meet my guest. He gets up from the chair by the window that overlooks the garden and walks towards me with his hand outstretched. Before I can ask him how his health is, he greets me warmly.

'It's good to see you again, Zander.' His words sound genuine and his handshake is firm. 'I hope you don't mind me addressing you by your first name. I am so sorry that our last meeting ended as it did. And I'm sorry about everything that followed that meeting. It's been a difficult time for both of us.'

I hadn't been sure what to expect when we came face to face and I'd run through a list of possible scenarios in my mind. But I hadn't anticipated that Damian Martyn would greet me like this. All of the things I'd imagined I might say at this moment seem utterly inappropriate and I'm at a loss as to how to respond. When I eventually manage to speak, my words are stumbling and hesitant.

'Well… if anyone should be apologising… I think it should be me.' The words *embarrassment* and *shame* are too weak to describe what I'm feeling at this moment, still holding the right hand and looking into the eyes of the man on whom such physical injury had been inflicted by my uncontrolled anger. 'I'd be insulting you and all you've been through in these last two years if I asked you to forgive me. But I am genuinely sorry. But let me ask how your health is now.'

He tells me that the first twelve months were challenging, but after that things began to slowly improve. Now, he assures me, he's almost back to how he was before, though he does get tired more quickly. I express my relief at this news and try to apologise again. Then there's an uncomfortable silence as I struggle to think what to say next. The best I can come up with is to invite him to take a seat so we can chat. Damian, however, has an alternative proposal.

'Actually, I've been looking out of the window. It's very peaceful out there. I know it holds bad memories for both of us, and this might sound a little odd. But, if you don't mind, I'd really like to sit out in the garden where we sat before. I think it might be a kind of catharsis for both of us.'

It's a request I wouldn't have anticipated, but since everything about this encounter feels odd to me, I readily concur with his suggestion. We make our way out to the patio and sit on either side of the little round wrought-iron table under the shade of the cherry trees. Neither of us seems quite sure how to pick up the conversation. We sit still for a time, content to breathe in the fresh air and listen to the birdsong. It's my visitor who speaks first again.

'I don't know about you,' he says, as his face slowly breaks into a smile. 'But I think I'd describe what I'm feeling right now as *déjà vu*…'

'Now, why does that worry me?' I ask. 'Let's hope that feeling doesn't extend to the rest of this afternoon.'

That opening exchange is enough to release the tension we're both feeling. We laugh together, albeit somewhat nervously. But I know it's time to get started and I turn my chair a little so I can look Damian in the face.

'So… we ought to talk. Why have you been so anxious to meet me? After our last encounter I assumed you'd never want to see me again.'

'Well, I certainly *have* been anxious to meet with you. And the first thing I need to say is that I *do* forgive you. That's not just me trying to take the moral high ground. Far from it. I'm the last person who should do that. But I

248

need to tell you what's been happening in my life since you were...'

He searches for a diplomatic phrase to describe my absence from society, so I quickly interject, 'Let's just call a spade a spade. You mean, since I was locked up in prison. Deservedly so, I'll admit. No need to beat around the bush.'

'OK, thanks. And the truth is that since you've been locked up in prison, I've been facing some challenging circumstances myself.'

I can tell from his expression that my initial suspicions that I might have unwisely put myself at the mercy of a wily reporter with a nasty trick up his sleeve are unfounded. It seems that he really does want to have a conversation rather than set some sort of trap for me to fall into. I listen closely as he continues.

'As you know, I'm generally regarded as a journalist who uncompromisingly separates the truth from the lies. That reputation has been hard-won and I've always been proud of it. I still believe that the first responsibility of anybody in my profession is to tell the truth, especially when there's any hint of a cover-up. But there are aspects of my work, and of my character for that matter, that I'm not so proud of. I've had to face up to the truth about myself in the last year as never before. And, if you don't mind listening, I'd like to share some of this stuff before I make a proposal to you.'

This conversation is moving in a direction that I definitely hadn't anticipated, but I assure him that if he thinks it's appropriate and helpful to talk to me about whatever is on his mind, then I'm willing to listen. We pause just long enough for Monica to set the coffee things on the table and fill our cups, before Damian launches into his tale.

'For a while I've been on the trail of a man – let's call him "Mr Jones" for the moment. He's the CEO of a charity working in developing countries. You know the kind of outfit – supporting organisations and groups working on the ground to implement sustainable initiatives that provide basic amenities for people in some of the poorest communities in the world. They're not one of the really big boys, but they do some worthwhile stuff, and they're generally well respected and trusted. They raise about £40 million a year, most of that from donations from the public. So, good PR is important to them. Well, I get the nod from a mate of mine who's an accountant and who's recently gone over their figures carefully that there's a sizeable hole in their accounts that nobody seems to be able to explain. The chief finance officer's the obvious suspect, but my accountant pal checks him out and he's clean. After a bit more digging around, he's pretty sure that it's the CEO.

'That's when he contacts me. He thinks this is my territory. You know – a highly respected individual who turns out to have feet of clay. Well, I do some initial enquiries. I enlist the help of an expert in the field of charity finances and the deeper we dig, the clearer it becomes that "Mr Jones" is our man. However, he doesn't fit the usual profile. His lifestyle isn't what you'd describe as affluent. If anything, his standard of living is surprisingly modest for somebody who comes from a fairly well-to-do middle-class family and has an income of £95,000 a year. Which makes it all the more intriguing, because we're pretty sure he's on the take. So, I decide to go after this guy. We track his movements, find out who his friends are, do a check on what he's spending his money on – that kind of thing. I've been at this game a long time. I've got a lot of contacts and I know how to keep our surveillance on the right side of the law, even if sometimes it's only just.'

He stops to take a sip of his coffee, swirling it round his mouth for what seems much longer than is normal before swallowing it. His eyes narrow as he puts his cup back on the table, and I sense that this is where the story is about to get more interesting.

'Turns out this guy is a tough nut to crack. I know things are not right and I'm sure he's been up to something, but I haven't got enough to go public. My editor looks at what I've managed to put together so far and he won't touch it. Says we could be on the wrong end of a lawsuit if we were to publish it without a lot more solid evidence. I'm figuring out where to go next with it. I even wonder if I should drop the story, when I get a call from "Mr Jones". Somebody's tipped him off that I'm investigating him and he wants to sit down and talk with me. So we meet in a motorway services off the M1 at eleven o'clock one night…'

That last little detail about meeting in a motorway services is enough for me to join the dots and put a face to the picture Damian's drawing. I chip in while he drinks the last of his coffee and pushes his cup aside.

'Your "Mr Jones" is really Rodney Brampton, the GlocalResponse CEO, isn't he?'

'You've got it.' He sighs and nods. 'And you know the end of the story. But I need to tell you what happened that night at the motorway services before he drove off…'

It takes Damian Martyn twenty minutes to tell the story of his late-night encounter with Rodney Brampton. There are moments when his emotions threaten to overcome him and he finds it hard to speak. More than once he interrupts the flow of his narrative with questions to himself as to why he hadn't responded differently or taken another course of action from the one he actually followed. At one point he gets up and walks round the garden as he gathers up his courage to carry on with his account of that fateful night. But I can give you the gist of his tale in a few sentences. You must imagine for yourself the impact of his tale when I hear it from his own lips.

Rodney Brampton had immediately admitted his guilt. He'd misappropriated almost a million pounds from GlocalResponse over the course of several years, somehow managing to cover his tracks and conceal the truth from the finance officer who was clearly overawed by his boss, and from the charity's accountants who were at best culpably negligent. His forthright confession immediately prompted an incredulous Damian Martyn to ask what had happened to the money as there was nothing in Brampton's lifestyle to offer any clue as to why he'd perpetrated such a large-scale fraud. The explanation of where the million pounds had gone – an explanation which further investigation proved to be absolutely true – left Damian open-mouthed with amazement at his naivety. Brampton had siphoned off the money into the account of another and quite separate aid agency, a practice that is, of course, strictly forbidden by charity law.

The answer to Damian's follow-up question as to why someone as experienced in the charity sector would do something as unethical and foolish as this solicited yet more surprising revelations. Brampton, who'd been married to his wife for twenty-five years and whose strong religious convictions are well known, disclosed that on one of his trips to Africa, he'd met a very attractive and vivacious woman, twenty years his junior, who was regarded as an up-and-coming star in the international aid sector. They'd embarked on a long-running affair. When a major project that she was heading up ran into what appeared to be temporary financial difficulties, he decided to indulge in what he described as 'a little bit of creative accounting' that would allow him to transfer money from GlocalResponse to shore up the project. It was intended to be a short-term and unofficial loan that would be quickly paid back. But things went from bad to worse with the project and, his infatuation with the woman getting the better of his judgement, he continued transferring money under the pretence that it was supporting various non-existing initiatives of GlocalResponse.

By the time they met that night, he'd already confessed his infidelity to his wife and broken off the relationship with the other woman. Even more to the point, his father had died a few months earlier, making him the sole beneficiary of his will and leaving him in a position to repay the total amount he'd misappropriated. He'd arranged with his lawyer to go to the police the following morning and make a full statement admitting exactly what had been going on. And his plea to Damian was that he should delay on publishing the story, or at least write it in a way that would minimise the damage that could be done to GlocalResponse, to his staff and to the people who relied on their help.

Damian reacted with scepticism. Was he being told the whole truth? Was this just a last-ditch attempt by Brampton, knowing his cover was blown, to emerge with some shred of credibility still intact? This was a man who'd paraded his religious principles while cheating on his wife and stealing from a charity to shore up his lover's reputation. A man who'd been lucky in getting hold of his inheritance at the right moment. There was no way he was going to let him off the hook. He remembers his last words to Brampton as he left the table to head back to his car.

'You're a cheat and a liar. You've got a cheek to ask for sympathy and understanding. I'm going make sure Britain knows the truth about you. And you can bet your life that I won't be pulling any punches.'

And he remembers exactly what Brampton had said to him in reply.

'Yes, I am a cheat and a liar. I've admitted that. But none of us is perfect. And I wonder how you'd come out of it if someone told the whole truth about you.'

I don't need my guest to tell me the end of the story. It was reported widely in the evening news the following day. Rodney Brampton left the motorway services and drove through the darkness to the Sussex coast where he parked his car and leapt to his death from the cliffs at Beachy Head.

Everything in my garden is just as it was when we began our conversation. The sun is still shining, the birds are still singing, the coffee cups are still lying on the table in front of us. But it's a full five minutes before either of us speaks again. I stay silent because I don't know what to say. Damian, I suspect, stays silent because he knows exactly what he has to say, what he has come to say. And it's difficult for him because he has never said it to anyone before.

'Zander, I told you when I got here that I *do* forgive you. And I forgive you, not just so I can feel smug about myself. Not just because it's the right thing to do. And not just because I have to rid myself of the bitter anger that I've felt towards you for too long. No, I forgive you because I'm in desperate need of forgiveness myself. And if there isn't any forgiveness, I'm totally stuffed.'

This is the man who sat in the same chair and looked at me across the same table almost two years ago to the day. But something has changed. *He is changed.* The person whose life and actions he is now intent on exposing to the light is himself.

'I'm haunted by Rodney Brampton's words. He was right. If someone told the truth about me, I wouldn't come out of it well. The only difference between me and Brampton is that he did what he did on a bigger stage. If I'd been in his situation, I might have done the same. Who knows? And when I look back on my life – all the expense accounts I've fiddled, all the corners I've cut to find out what I wanted to know, all the folk I've paid to pick up the dirt on people they knew, all the women I've slept with and discarded, all the lies I've told my wife – I don't like what I see. And worst of all, I've done it all while taking the moral high ground. The intrepid reporter who ferrets out the facts, who fearlessly exposes the truth. And now, because I didn't have the humanity to show a little bit of compassion towards a broken man, I'll have his death on my conscience for the rest of my life.'

He looks at me, his eyes pleading for an answer that will give him some hope.

'I don't know why I'm asking you, of all people. But I don't know who else to ask. And if someone doesn't tell me that I can be forgiven, I don't know how I will carry this.'

For the second time in my life I find myself in the place where I have the awesome and humbling responsibility – a responsibility that is unsought and undeserved – of hearing the confession of a man who needs to be absolved from the guilt that is burdening him. But unlike the vigil I kept by the bedside of Byron Abercrombie-Brydges, a man to whom I had been a good friend, I am now sitting in my garden listening to the confession of a man I have deeply wronged. And for the first time in my life, I see clearly the depth of the enigma that has been confronting me for so long, the paradox that I cannot escape. In this tragicomedy that is life on this planet, I am cast in a dual role. I am both sinner in need of forgiveness and priest who must offer that same forgiveness to everyone who seeks it from me. To fail to play either of those parts is to be less than truly human.

The problem is that it's like asking a five-year-old child to play the part of King Lear or Othello. Just like that child, I have neither the maturity nor the resources to take on such demanding roles. But, at this moment, face to face with a man who desperately needs to be forgiven, I remember #ISoFaS and I pray to whoever might be listening that the words Alan Kibbell wrote on his arm in a prison visiting hall are more than just a neat slogan dreamed up by a trendy vicar. If there really is an inexhaustible source of forgiveness and strength, then I need it right now.

Summoning up my energy, I push the wrought-iron table that separates us to one side. I stand up, beckon to Damian to do the same, and throw my arms around him. We embrace each other for long minutes, two middle-aged men in need of forgiveness. The tears are streaming down our faces, as I repeat the same words over and over again.

'Yes, Damian, you can be forgiven. You *are* forgiven. And I forgive you. Please forgive me.'

future

chapter 21
let me tell you a story
2015 and beyond

I walk back up the path to my front door having watched Damian Martyn drive off. We have pledged to meet regularly for the next six months. Together we've resolved to explore a land hitherto little regarded by us, but now the place where we long to spend our days. We are determined to breathe its pure air, to harvest its finest fruits, to study its greatest wonders and to mine the incomparable riches that lie hidden beneath its soil. Having spent too long in a realm where ambition and wealth have been the coinage and where our souls have grown hard and dry, we are travelling to a place where business is transacted solely in the currency of humility and apology and forgiveness.

As soon as I close the door behind me, I pick up the phone and call Alan Kibbell. He has the air of a man who has sojourned in this land with which we two are unfamiliar. I ask him if he will be our guide as we take our first steps into what for us is virgin territory. He confesses himself to be still inexpert in navigating through this landscape, and he warns me that the terrain is often challenging. But he agrees to accompany us, and adds that he's happy to travel with us. It is, he says knowingly, a journey best done in good company.

Then I spend the evening with my wife and son, feeling grateful for them both. We tuck Alexander William Bennings into bed and watch him as he falls asleep. He will be the fifth male in this family to carry the name Alexander. He will, I hope, live well and grow old in a world I will not see. He will make his own choices, good and bad, and he will have to discover for himself the forgiveness and strength that the generations who have gone before him have sometimes sought and found and sometimes lost, or thrown carelessly away.

Monica and I sit talking into the evening as I relate the details of my meeting with Damian earlier in the day. She's not surprised by anything I tell her, seeming to know it before I put it into words. I'm impressed by what I assume is her female intuition and insightfulness until she admits with a smile that she'd left the kitchen window ajar so that she could observe everything as it happened.

'Well,' she says snuggling up to me on the couch. 'You don't think I'd want you to face a meeting like that without staying close enough to help in case you needed me.'

Monica switches off the television after we've watched the ten o'clock news and suggests that since it's been an emotionally tiring day, it's time for bed. Normally she's a little concerned when I say that I'm going to stay up late. But when I tell her that I want to start work on a new book, she's delighted.

'Oh, good. This is the first time you've wanted to write since you came home from prison. You've got an idea for another novel?'

'No, not a novel this time. I think I want to write the story of my family. Four generations, four Alexanders. How our lives have all been so different, but how in the end we've all been looking for the same thing. And I think I've got a title and the first couple of paragraphs.'

I kiss my wife goodnight and go through to my study where I sit at my desk and think for a moment. Then I begin to type:

TO THE FOURTH GENERATION
Chapter 1: the golden trowel
I've been telling stories all my life. That's what I do. That's what I've always done. It must have started with the squiggles and scribbled drawings I made of what I could see around me when I was very young...

resources

Chapter 2
Relating to outbreak of the First World War:
https://www.bl.uk/world-war-one/articles/origins-and-outbreak (accessed 20th May 2020).

Relating to events in the chapter:
http://robertson-gray.org.uk/world-war-one/essay-competition.php
https://www.iwm.org.uk/history/voices-of-the-first-world-war-over-by-christmas
https://www.iwm.org.uk/history/voices-of-the-first-world-war-trench-life
(all accessed March–April 2020).

Note:
The First, Second and Third Battalions of the Highland Light Infantry were later renamed/renumbered the Fifteenth, Sixteenth and Seventeenth Battalions. For the purpose of simplicity and to avoid confusion I have kept the original numberings.

Chapter 3

http://ww1centenary.oucs.ox.ac.uk/body-and-mind/lloyd-georges-ministry-men/ (accessed 4th May 2020).

Chapter 4

Donald Southgate (ed), *The Conservative Leadership*, 1832-1932 (London: Macmillan 1974), p213.
Jim Connell (1852-1929), 'The Red Flag', https://www.marxists.org/subject/art/music/lyrics/en/red-flag.htm (accessed 19th April 2020).
Sabine Baring-Gould (1834-1924), 'Onward, Christian Soldiers', https://www.hymnal.net/en/hymn/h/871 (accessed 15th May 2020).
Elisha Albright Hoffman (1839-1929), 'Have You Been to Jesus for the Cleansing Power', https://www.hymnal.net/en/hymn/h/1007 (accessed 27th April 2020).

Chapter 5

Robert Burns (1759-96), 'A Man's a Man for a' That', https://www.scottishpoetrylibrary.org.uk/poem/mans-man-0/ (accessed 14th April 2020).
Thomas Henry Huxley (1825-95) in *The Times*, 1890, 'corybantic Christianity', http://www.worldwidewords.org/weirdwords/ww-cor1.htm (accessed 1st May 2020).
Junior soldier's promise, https://www.salvationarmy.org/ihq/5685B006CB0C3AC7802573750042401C (accessed 21st May 2020).

Chapters 8 & 19

George Gordon Byron (Lord Byron), 1788-1824, *Childe Harold's Pilgrimage*, in *The Works of Lord Byron*, Volume One (London: John Murray, 1815), p253.

Chapter 9

Edvard Munch quote, https://www.visitoslo.com/en/osloregion/articles-new/five-fun-things-about-edvard-munch/ (accessed 20th April 2020).

Charlie Parker Salvation Army Band in New York incident: Gary Giddins, *Celebrating Bird: The Triumph of Charlie Parker* (Minneapolis, MN: University of Minnesota Press, 2013).

Chapter 13

Robert Burns (1759-96), 'My Love is Like a Red, Red Rose', https://www.scottishpoetrylibrary.org.uk/poem/red-red-rose/ (accessed 20th April 2020).

Chapter 19

Lewis Carroll, *Alice's Adventure in Wonderland* (London: Macmillan, 1865).

Also by Chick Yuill:

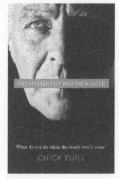

Meet Matthew Gold: wealthy, successful and secure – but totally alone. Afflicted from childhood by a crippling stammer, words have been his greatest problem. But, as his talent as a writer of detective fiction emerges, words become his greatest passion. He might struggle to speak, but on the pages of his novels his slick-talking private eye knows all the answers and can always find the words to illuminate every mystery.

But what happens when life itself becomes a mystery you cannot solve? What do you say and what can you do when words come to an end?

Instant Apostle, 2019, ISBN 978-1-909728-65-3

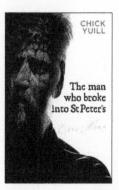

When the caretaker of St Peter's finds that the church has been broken into early on the Saturday morning after Christmas and that the elderly intruder is still in the building and kneeling at the communion rail, no one is quite sure what to do.

But the confusion caused by the sudden arrival of this unexpected visitor is as nothing compared to the impact of his continuing presence on the church and the town. As his identity becomes clear and his story unfolds, long-hidden truths emerge, and life in Penford can never be quite the same again…

Instant Apostle, 2018, ISBN 978-1-909728-87-5

Where can a man find grace when he no longer believes? Ray Young has been married for almost thirty years. But his once vibrant faith, like his marriage, is steadily fading, and relations with his only son Ollie are increasingly strained. Facing this looming crisis of faith, Ray begins an affair, only for Ollie to discover his father's infidelity. Confronted by his actions, Ray has one chance to rescue the life that is crumbling around him. But when tragedy strikes, it seems all hope of redemption is gone…

Instant Apostle, 2017, ISBN 978-1-909728-65-3